The Casta Flag

Jules Gabriel Verne

Volume 47 of 54 in the

"Voyages Extraordinaires"

First published in 1900.

2014 Reprint by Kassock Bros. Publishing Co.

Printed in the United States Of America

Cover Illustration By Isaac M. Kassock

ISBN: 1495300862
ISBN-13: 978-1495300868

Jules Gabriel Verne (1828-1905)

The Extraordinary Voyages
of
Jules Verne

~

01 - Five Weeks in a Balloon

02 - The Adventures of Captain Hatteras

03 - Journey to the Center of the Earth

04 - From the Earth to the Moon

05 - In Search of the Castaways

06 - Twenty Thousand Leagues Under the Sea

07 - Around The Moon

08 - A Floating City

09 - The Adventures of Three Englishmen and Three Russians in South Africa

10 - The Fur Country

11 - Around the World in Eighty Days

12 - The Mysterious Island

13 - The Survivors of the *Chancellor*

14 - Michael Strogoff

15 - Off on a Comet

16 - The Child of the Cavern

17 – A Captain at Fifteen

18 - The Begum's Millions

19 - Tribulations of a Chinaman in China

20 - The Steam House

21 - Eight Hundred Leagues on the Amazon

22 - Godfrey Morgan

23 - The Green Ray

24 - Kéraban the Inflexible

25 - The Vanished Diamond

26 - The Archipelago on Fire

27 - Mathias Sandorf

Table of Contents

THE CASTAWAYS OF THE FLAG

Jules Verne

Chapter I - The Castaways

Night-a pitch-dark night! It was almost impossible to distinguish sky from sea. From the sky, laden with clouds low and heavy, deformed and tattered, lightning flashed every now and then, followed by muffled rolls of thunder. At these flashes the horizon lit up for a moment and showed deserted and melancholy.

No wave broke in foam upon the surface of the sea. There was nothing but the regular and monotonous rolling of the swell and the gleam of ripples under the lightning flashes. Not a breath moved across the vast plain of ocean, not even the hot breath of the storm. But electricity so charged the atmosphere that it escaped in phosphorescent light, and ran up and down the rigging of the boat in tongues of Saint Elmo's fire. Although the sun had set four or five hours ago, the sweltering heat of the day had not passed. Two men talked in low tones, in the stern of a big ship's boat that was decked in to the foot of the mast. Her foresail and jib were flapping as the monotonous rolling shook her.

One of these men, holding the tiller tucked under his arm, tried to dodge the cruel swell that rolled the boat from side to side. He was a sailor, about forty years of age, thick-set and sturdy, with a frame of iron on which fatigue, privation, even despair, had never taken effect. An Englishman by nationality, this boatswain was named John Block.

The other man was barely eighteen, and did not seem to belong to the sea-faring class.

In the bottom of the boat, under the poop and seats, with no strength left to pull the oars, a number of human beings were lying, among them a child of five years old-a poor little creature whose whimpering was audible, whom its mother tried to hush with idle talk and kisses.

Before the mast, upon the poop, and near the jib stays, two people sat motionless and silent, hand in hand, lost in the most gloomy thoughts. So intense was the darkness that it was only by the lightning flashes that they could see each other.

From the bottom of the boat a head was lifted sometimes, only to droop again at once.

The Castaways of the Flag

The boatswain spoke to the young man lying by his side.

"No, no. I watched the horizon until the sun went down. No land in sight-not a sail! But what I didn't see this evening will perhaps be visible at dawn."

"But, bo'sun," his companion answered, "we must get to land somewhere in the next forty-eight hours, or we shall have succumbed."

"That's true," John Block agreed. "Land must appear-simply must. Why, continents and islands were made on purpose to give shelter to brave men, and one always ends by getting to them!"

"If the wind helps one, bo'sun."

"That is the only reason wind was invented," John Block replied. "Today, as bad luck would have it, it was busy somewhere else, in the middle of the Atlantic or the Pacific perhaps, for it didn't blow enough here to fill my cap. Yes, a jolly good gale would blow us merrily along."

"Or swallow us up, Block."

"Oh no, not that! No, no, not that! Of all ways to bring this job to a finish, that would be the worst."

"Who can tell, bo'sun?"

Then for some minutes the two men were silent. Nothing could be heard but the gentle rippling under the boat.

"How is the captain?" the young man went on.

"Captain Gould, good man, is in bad case," John Block replied. "How those blackguards knocked him about! The wound in his head makes him cry out with pain. And it was an officer in whom he had every confidence who stirred those wretches up! No, no! One fine morning, or one fine afternoon, or perhaps one fine evening, that rascal of a Borupt shall make his last ugly face at the yardarm or-"

"The brute! The brute!" the young man exclaimed, clenching his fists in wrath. "But poor Harry Gould! You dressed his wounds this evening, Block-"

"Ay, ay; and when I put him back under the poop, after I had put compresses on his head, he was able to speak to me, though very feebly. 'Thanks, Block, thanks,' he said-as if I wanted thanks! 'And land? What about land?' he asked. 'You may be quite sure, captain,' I told him, 'that there is land somewhere, and perhaps not very far off.' He looked at me and closed his eyes."

And the boatswain murmured in an aside: "Land! Land! Ah, Borupt and his accomplices knew very well what they were about! While we were shut up in the bottom of the hold, they altered the course; they went some hundreds of miles away before they cast us adrift in this boat-in seas where a ship is hardly ever seen, I guess."

The young man had risen. He stooped, listening to port.

"Didn't you hear anything, Block?" he asked.

"Nothing, nothing at all," the boatswain answered; "this swell is as noiseless as if it were made of oil instead of water."

The young man said no more, but sat down again with his arms folded across his breast.

Just at this moment one of the passengers sat up, and exclaimed, with a gesture of despair: "I wish a wave would smash this boat up, and swallow us all up with it, rather than that we should all be given over to the horrors of starvation! Tomorrow we shall have exhausted the last of our provisions. We shall have nothing left at all."

"Tomorrow is tomorrow, Mr. Wolston," the boatswain replied. "If the boat were to capsize there wouldn't be any tomorrow for us; and while there is a tomorrow-"

"John Block is right," his young companion answered. "We must not give up hope, James! Whatever danger threatens us, we are in God's hands, to dispose of as He thinks fit. His hand is in all that comes to us, and it is not right to say that He has withdrawn it from us."

"I know," James whispered, drooping his head, "but one is not always master of one's self."

Another passenger, a man of about thirty, one of those who had been sitting in the bows, approached John Block and said:

The Castaways of the Flag

"Bo'sun, since our unfortunate captain was thrown into this boat with us-and that is a week ago already-it is you who have taken his place. So our lives are in your hands. Have you any hope?"

"Have I any hope?" John Block replied. "Yes! I assure you I have. I hope these infernal calms will come to an end shortly and that the wind will take us safe to harbor."

"Safe to harbor!" the passenger answered, his eyes trying to pierce the darkness of the night.

"Well, what the deuce!" John Block exclaimed. "There is a harbor somewhere! All we have to do is to steer for it, with the wind whistling through the yards. Good Lord! If I were the Creator I would show you half a dozen islands lying all round us, waiting our convenience!"

"We won't ask for as many as that, bo'sun," the passenger replied, unable to refrain from smiling.

"Well," John Block answered, "if He will drive our boat towards one of those which exist already, it will be enough, and He need not make any islands on purpose, although, I must say, He seems to have been a bit stingy with them hereabouts!"

"But where are we?"

"I can't tell you, not even within a few hundred miles," John Block replied. "You know that for a whole long week we were shut up in the hold, unable to see what course the ship was shaping, whether south or north. Any how, it must have been blowing steadily, and the sea did plenty of rolling and chopping."

"That is true, John Block, and true, too, that we must have gone a long way; but in what direction?"

"About that I don't know anything," the boatswain declared. "Did the ship go off to the Pacific, instead of making for the Indian Ocean? On the day of the mutiny we were off Madagascar. But since then, as the wind has blown from the west all the time, we may have been taken hundreds of miles from there, towards the islands of Saint Paul and Amsterdam."

"Where there are none but savages of the worst possible sort," James Wolston remarked. "But after all, the men who cast us away are not much better."

"One thing is certain," John Block declared; "that wretch Borupt must have altered the *Flag's* course and made for waters where he will be most likely to escape punishment, and where he and his gang will play pirates! So I think that we were a long way out of our proper course when this boat was put adrift. But I wish we might strike some island in these seas-even a desert island would do! We could live all right by hunting and fishing; we should find shelter in some cave. Why shouldn't we make of our island what the survivors of the *Landlord* made of

New Switzerland? With strong arms, brains, and pluck-"

"Very true," James Wolston answered, "but the *Landlord* did not fail her passengers. They were able to save her cargo, while we shall never have anything from the *Flag's* cargo."

The conversation was interrupted. A voice that rang with pain was heard:

"Drink! Give me something to drink!"

"It's Captain Gould," one of the passengers said. "He is eaten up with fever. Luckily there is plenty of water, and-"

"That's my job," said the boatswain. "Do one of you take the tiller. I know where the can is, and a few mouthfuls will give the captain ease."

And John Block left his seat aft and went forward into the bows of the boat.

The three other passengers remained in silence, awaiting his return.

After being away for two or three minutes John Block came back to his post.

"Well?" someone inquired.

"Someone got there before me," John Block answered. "One of our good angels was with the patient already, pouring a little fresh water between his lips, and bathing his forehead that was wet with sweat. I don't know whether Captain Gould was conscious. He seemed to be delirious. He was talking about land. 'The land ought to be over there,' he kept saying, and his hand was wobbling about like the pennon on the mainmast when all winds are blowing at once. I answered: 'Ay, ay, captain, quite so. The land is somewhere! We shall reach it soon. I can smell it, to northwards.' And that is a sure thing. We old sailors can smell land like that. And I said too: 'Don't be uneasy, captain, everything is all right. We have a stout boat and I will keep her course steady. There must be more islands hereabouts than we could know what to do with. Too many to choose from! We shall find one to suit our convenience-an inhabited island where we shall find a welcome and where we shall be sent home from.' The poor chap understood what I said, I am sure, and when I held the lantern near his face he smiled to me-such a sad smile!-and at the good angel too. Then he closed his eyes again, and fell asleep almost at once. Well! I may have lied pretty heavily when I talked about land to him as if it were only a few miles off, but was I far wrong!'

"No, Block," the youngest passenger replied; "that is the kind of lie that God allows."

The conversation ended, and the silence was only broken thereafter by the flapping of the sail against the mast as the boat rolled from one side to the other. Most of those who were aboard her, broken down by fatigue and weakened by long privation, forgot their terrors in heavy sleep.

Although these unhappy people still had something wherewith to quench their thirst, they would have nothing wherewith to appease their hunger in the coming days. Of the few pounds of salt meat that had been flung into the boat when she was pushed off, nothing now remained. They were reduced to one bag of sea-biscuits for eleven people. How could they manage, if the calm persisted? And for the last forty-eight hours not one breath of breeze had stolen through the stifling atmosphere, not even one of those intermittent gusts which are like the last sighs of a dying man. It meant death by starvation, and that within a short time.

There was no steam navigation in those days. So the probability was that, in the absence of wind, no ship would come into sight, and, in the absence of wind, the boat could not reach land, whether island or continent.

Jules Verne

It was necessary to have perfect faith in God to combat utter despair, or else to possess the unshakeable philosophy of the boatswain, which consisted in refusing to see any but the bright side of things. Even now he muttered to himself:

"Ay, ay, I know; the time will come when the last biscuit will have been eaten; but as long as one can keep one's stomach one mustn't grumble, even if there is nothing to put in it! Now, if one hadn't got a stomach left, even if there were plenty to put in it-that would be really serious!"

Two hours passed. The boat had not moved a cable's length, for there was only the motion of the swell to affect her. Now the swell does not move forward; it merely makes the surface of the water undulate. A few chips of wood that had been thrown over the side the day before were still floating close by, and the sail had not filled once to move the boat away from them.

While merely afloat like this, it was little use to remain at the helm. But the boatswain declined to leave his post. With the tiller under his arm, he tried at least to avoid the lurching which tilted the boat to one side and another, and thus to spare his companions excessive shaking.

It was about three o'clock in the morning when John Block felt a light breath pass across his cheeks, roughened and hardened as they were by the salt sea air.

"Can the wind be getting up?" he murmured as he rose.

He turned towards the south, and, wetting his finger in his mouth, held it up. There was a distinct sensation of coldness, caused by the evaporation, and now a distant rippling sound became audible.

He turned to the passenger sitting on the middle bench, near one of the women.

"Mr. Fritz!" he said.

Fritz Robinson raised his head and bent round.

"What do you want, bo'sun?" he asked.

"Look over there-towards the east."

"What do you think you see?"

12

The Castaways of the Flag

"If I'm not mistaken, a kind of rift, like a belt, on the water-line."

Unmistakably there was a lighter line along the horizon in that direction. Sky and sea could be distinguished with more definiteness. It was as if a rent had just been made in the dome of mist and vapor

"It's wind!" the boatswain declared.

"Isn't it only the first beginning of daybreak?" the passenger asked.

"It might be daylight, though it's very early for it," John Block replied, "and again it might be a breeze! I felt something of it in my beard just now, and look! It's twitching still! I'm aware it's not a breeze to fill the top-gallant sails, but anyhow it's more than we've had for the last four and twenty hours. Put your hand to your ear, Mr. Fritz, and listen; you'll hear what I heard."

"You are right," said the passenger, leaning over the gunwale; "it is the breeze."

"And we're ready for it," the boatswain replied, "with the foresail block and tackle. We've only got to haul the sheet taut to save all the wind which is rising."

"But where will it take us?"

"Wherever it likes," the boatswain answered; "all I want it to do is to blow us out of these cursed waters!"

Twenty minutes went by. The breath of wind, which at first was almost imperceptible, grew stronger. The rippling aft became louder. The boat made a few rougher motions, not caused by the slow, nauseating swell. Folds of the sail spread out, fell flat, and opened again, and the sheet sagged against its cleats. The wind was not strong enough yet to fill the heavy canvas of the foresail and the jib. Patience was needed, while the boat's head was kept to her course as well as might be by means of one of the sculls.

A quarter of an hour later, progress was marked by a light wake.

Just at this moment one of the passengers who had been lying in the bows got up and looked at the rift in the clouds to the eastward.

"Is it a breeze?" he asked.

"Yes," John Block answered. "I think we have got it this time, like a bird in the hand and we won't let go of it!"

The wind was beginning to spread steadily now through the rift, through which, too, the first gleams of light must come. From southeast to south-west, the clouds still hung in heavy masses, over three-quarters of the circumference of the sky. It was still impossible to see more than a few cables' lengths from the boat, and beyond that distance no ship could have been detected.

As the breeze had freshened, the sheet had to be hauled in, the foresail, whose gear was slackened, hoisted, and the course veered a point or two, so as to give the jib a hold on the wind.

"We've got it; we've got it!" the boatswain said cheerily, and the boat, heeling gently over to starboard, dipped her nose into the first waves.

Little by little the rent in the clouds grew bigger and spread overhead. The sky assumed a reddish hue. It seemed that the wind might hold to the present quarter for some little time, and that the period of calms had come to an end.

Hope of reaching land revived once more, or the alternative hope of falling in with a ship.

At five o'clock the rent in the clouds was ringed with a collar of vivid colored clouds. It was the day, appearing with the suddenness peculiar to the low latitudes of the tropical regions. Soon purple rays of light arose above the horizon, like the sticks of a fan. The rim of the solar disc, heightened by the refraction, touched the horizon line, drawn clearly now at the end of sky and sea. At once the rays of light caught on the little clouds which hung in the high heaven, and dyed them every shade of crimson. But they were stubbornly arrested by the dense vapors accumulated in the north, and could not break through them. And so the range of vision, long behind, was still extremely limited in front. The boat was leaving a long wake behind her now, marked in creamy white upon the greenish water.

And now the whole sun emerged above the horizon, enormously magnified at its diameter. No haze dimmed its brilliance, which was insupportable to the eye. All aboard the boat looked away from it; they only scanned the north, whither the wind was carrying them. The main question was what the fog screened from them in that direction.

The Castaways of the Flag

At length, just before half-past six, one of the passengers seized the halyards of the foresail and clambered nimbly up to the yardarm, just as the sun cleared the sky to the eastward with its early rays.

And in a ringing voice he shouted:

"Land!"

Jules Verne

Chapter II - In England

It was on the 20th of October that the *Unicorn* had left New Switzerland on her way back to England. On her return, when the Admiralty sent to take possession of the new colony in the Indian Ocean, after a brief stop at the Cape of Good Hope, she was to bring back Fritz and Frank Zermatt, Jenny Montrose and Dolly Wolston. The two brothers took the berths left vacant by the Wolstons who were now settled on the island. A comfortable cabin had been placed at the disposal of Jenny and her little companion Dolly, who was going to join James Wolston and his wife and child at Cape Town.

After rounding the False Hope Point the *Unicorn* sailed westward before the wind and came down to the south again, leaving the island of Burning Rock to her starboard. Before finally leaving New Switzerland Lieutenant Littlestone decided to reconnoitre its eastern coast as well, in order to satisfy himself that it really was an isolated island in these seas, and to form an approximate idea of the size of a colony which would soon be included among the island dominions of Great Britain. As soon as he had done this, the corvette, with a fair wind behind her, left the island to the north-west, after getting little more than a glimpse of its southern portion through the haze and fog.

Fortune favored the first few weeks of the voyage. The passengers on the *Unicorn* were delighted with the weather, as well as with the cordial treatment which they received from the commander and the other officers. When they all met at table in the officers' mess, or under the awning on the poop, the conversation generally turned upon the wonders of New Switzerland. If the corvette met with nothing to delay her they all hoped to see it again within the year.

Fritz and Jenny often talked of Colonel Montrose, and of the gladness that would be his when be clasped in his arms the daughter whom he had thought he would never see again. For three years no news had been received of the *Dorcas,* whose loss with nearly all hands had been confirmed, by the survivors who had been taken to Sydney. But when they reached England Jenny would present to her father the man who had rescued her, and would beg him to bless their union.

The Castaways of the Flag

As for Frank, though Dolly Wolston was only fourteen, it would not be without a bitter pang that he would leave her at Cape Town, and keen would be his longing to come back to her side!

After crossing the Tropic, off the Isle of France, the *Unicorn* encountered less favorable winds. These delayed her arrival at her port until the 17th of December, two months after her departure from New Switzerland.

The corvette came to anchor in the harbor of Cape Town, where she was to remain for a week.

One of the first visitors to come aboard was James Wolston. He knew that his father, mother, and two sisters had taken passages on the *Unicorn,* and his disappointment can be imagined at finding that there was only one sister for him to meet. Dolly presented Fritz and Frank Zermatt to him.

"Your father and mother and sister Hannah are living in New Switzerland now, Mr. Wolston," Fritz told him; "an unknown island on which my family was cast twelve years ago, after the wreck of the *Landlord.* They have decided to remain there and expect you to join them. When she comes back from Europe the *Unicorn* will take you and your wife and child to our island, if you are willing to go with us."

"When is the corvette due back at the Cape?" James Wolston inquired.

"In eight or nine months," Fritz replied, "and she will go from here to New Switzerland where the British flag will be flying. My brother Frank and I have availed ourselves of this opportunity to take back to London the daughter of Colonel Montrose who, we hope, will consent to come and settle with her in our second fatherland."

"And with you too, Fritz dear; for you will have become his son," Jenny added, giving him her hand.

"That is my most ardent wish, Jenny dear," said Fritz.

"And we and our parents do very much want you to bring your family and settle in New Switzerland," Dolly Wolston added.

"You must insist on the fact, Dolly," Frank declared, "that our island is the most wonderful island that has ever appeared above the sea."

"James will be the first to agree, when he has seen it," Dolly answered. "When once you have set foot in New Switzerland, and stayed at Rock Castle-"

"And roosted at Falconhurst, eh, Dolly?" said Jenny, laughing.

"Yes, roosted," the little girl replied; "well, then you will never want to leave New Switzerland again!"

"You hear Mr. Wolston?" said Fritz.

"I hear, M. Zermatt," James Wolston answered.

"To settle in your island and open up its first commercial relations with Great Britain is a proposition that I find peculiarly inviting. My wife and I will talk about it, and if we decide to go we will wind up our affairs and hold ourselves in readiness to em bark upon the *Unicorn* when she comes back to Cape Town. I am sure Susan will not hesitate."

"I will do whatever my husband wishes," Mrs. Wolston said.

Fritz and Frank shook James Wolston's hand warmly as Dolly kissed her sister-in-law.

"While the corvette stays here," James Wolston then explained, "we expect you all to accept the hospitality of our house. That will be the best way to knit our friendship, and we will talk as much as you please about New Switzerland."

Naturally the passengers on the *Unicorn* accepted this invitation in the spirit in which it had been offered.

An hour later Mr. and Mrs. James Wolston received their guests. Fritz and Frank were given a room between them, and Jenny shared the one allotted to Dolly, as she had shared her cabin during the voyage.

Mrs. James Wolston was a young woman of twenty-four, gentle, intelligent, and devoted to her husband. He was an earnest and active man, very much like his father. They had one boy, Bob, now five years old, whom they adored.

During the ten days that the *Unicorn* remained in the port, from the 17th to the 27th of December, little was talked about but New Switzerland, the events of which it had been the stage, the various works undertaken, and the many contrivances and improvements effected on the island. The subject was never exhausted. Dolly would expatiate on all these wonderful things, and Frank would encourage her to go on, and even find fault with her for not saying enough. Then Jenny Montrose would embroider the tale, to Fritz's keen delight.

In a word, the time sped, and James Wolston and his wife quite made up their minds to leave the Cape for New Switzerland. During the voyage of the corvette home and out again, Wolston would employ himself winding up his affairs and realizing his capital; he would be ready to start directly the *Unicorn* reappeared; and he would be one of the first emigrants to the island.

The last good-byes had to be said at length, with the comforting reflection that in another eight or nine months they would be at Cape Town again, and that then they would all put to sea together, outward bound for New Switzerland. Nevertheless, the parting was a painful one. Jenny Montrose and Susan Wolston mingled their kisses and tears, to which Dolly's were added. The child was much distressed by Frank's departure, and his heart, too, was heavy, for he had grown very fond of her. As he and his brother clasped James Wolston's hand they could assure themselves that they were leaving there a true friend indeed.

The *Unicorn* put to sea on the 27th, in somewhat overcast weather. Her passage was of average length. For several weeks winds varied from north-west to south-west. The corvette spoke Saint Helena, Ascension, and the Cape Verde Islands. Then, after passing in sight of the Canaries and Azores, off the coasts of Portugal and France, she came up the Channel, rounded the Isle of Wight, and, on the 14th of February, dropped anchor at Portsmouth.

Jenny Montrose wanted to start at once for London, where her aunt lived. If the Colonel were on active service she would not find him there, since the campaign for which he had been recalled from India might have lasted for several years. But if he had retired, he would have settled near his sister-in-law, and it would be there that he would at length set eyes again upon her whom he believed to have perished in the wreck of the *Dorcas*.

Fritz and Frank offered to escort Jenny to London, whither business called them also, and Fritz naturally wanted to meet Colonel Montrose soon. So all three set out the same evening, and arrived in London during the morning of the 23rd.

But bitter grief fell upon Jenny Montrose. She learned from her aunt that the colonel had died during his last campaign, without the happiness of knowing that the daughter whom he had mourned for was still alive.

After coming back from the far waters of the Indian Ocean to embrace her father, hoping never to part from him again, to present her savior to him, and to beg for his consent to their union and his blessing on it, Jenny would never see him more!

Her distress was great. In vain her aunt lavished on her words of consolation; in vain Fritz sorrowed with her. The blow was too cruel. She had never even thought of the possibility that her father might be dead.

A few days later, in a conversation broken by tears and regrets, Jenny said to. him:

"Fritz, dear Fritz, we have just experienced the bitterest of misfortunes, you and I. If you have not changed your mind at all-"

"Oh, Jenny, my darling!" Fritz exclaimed.

"Yes, I know," said Jenny, "and my father would have been happy to call you his son. I am sure he would have wanted to go with us and share our life in the new English colony. But I must give up that happiness. I am alone in the world now, and have only myself to depend upon! Alone? No, no! You are there, Fritz."

"Jenny," said the young man, "the whole of my life shall be devoted to your happiness."

"And mine to yours, Fritz dear! But since my father is no longer here to give us his consent, since I have no near relations living, and since yours is the only family I can call my own-"

"You have belonged to it three years already, Jenny dear, ever since the day when I found you on Burning Rock."

"I love them all, and they love me, Fritz! Well, in a few months more we shall be with them all again; we shall be back-"

"Married, Jenny?"

The Castaways of the Flag

"Yes, Fritz, if you wish it, since you have your father's consent and my aunt will not refuse me hers."

"Jenny, dear Jenny!" Fritz exclaimed, falling on his knees beside her. "Our plans will not be changed at all, and I shall take back my wife to my father and mother."

Jenny Montrose remained henceforth in her aunt's house, where Fritz and Frank came every day to see her. Meanwhile all the necessary arrangements were made for the celebration of the marriage within the briefest time that the law permitted.

But there was other business of some importance to be attended to, business which had been the purpose of the two brothers in coming to Europe.

There was the sale of the various articles of value collected on the island, the coral gathered on Whale Island, the pearls taken from the bay, the nutmegs and the vanilla. M. Zermatt had not been mistaken about their market value. They produced the considerable sum of eight thousand pounds sterling.

When one remembered that the banks of Pearl Bay had been no more than skimmed, that coral was to be found on many parts of the coast, that nutmegs and vanilla could be produced in large quantities, and that there were many other treasures in New Switzerland, one had to acknowledge that the colony was destined for a height of prosperity which set it in the foremost of the over-sea dominions of Great Britain.

In accordance with M. Zermatt's instructions part of the sum realized from the sale of these articles was to be spent upon things required to complete the stock at Rock Castle and the farms in the Promised Land. The rest, about three-quarters of the whole sum, and the ten thousand pounds coming from Colonel Montrose's estate, were deposited in the Bank of England, upon which M. Zermatt would be able to draw in the future as he might require, thanks to the communication which would soon be established with the capital.

Restitution was made of the various jewels and monies belonging to the families of those who had been lost with the *Landlord*, who had been traced after inquiry. Finally, a month after the arrival of Fritz Zermatt and Jenny Montrose in London, their marriage was celebrated there by the chaplain of the corvette. The *Unicorn* had brought them as

21

an engaged couple, and would take them back to New Switzerland a married couple.

All these events excited a considerable interest throughout Great Britain in the family which had been abandoned for a dozen years on an unknown island in the Indian Ocean, and in Jenny's adventures and her stay on Burning Rock. The story which had been written by Jean Zermatt appeared in the English and foreign newspapers, and under the title of "The Swiss Family Robinson," it was destined to a fame equal to that won already by the immortal work of Daniel Defoe.

The consequence of all this was that the Admiralty decided to take possession of New Switzerland. Moreover, this new possession had some very considerable advantages to offer. The island occupied an important position in the east of the Indian Ocean, near the entrance to the Sunda seas, on the road to the Far East. Seven hundred and fifty miles at most separated it from the western coast of Australia. The sixth part of the world, discovered by the Dutch in 1605, visited by Abel Tasman in 1644 and by Captain Cook in 1774, was destined to become one of England's principal dominions. Thus the Admiralty could but congratulate itself on its acquisition of an island so near that continent.

And thus the dispatch of the *Unicorn* to its waters was decided upon. The corvette would set out again in a few months under the command of Lieutenant Littlestone, promoted captain on this occasion. Fritz and Jenny Zermatt were to sail in her with Frank, and also a few colonists, pending the time when other emigrants, in larger numbers, would sail in other ships to the same destination.

It was arranged that the corvette should put in at the Cape to pick up James and Susan and Dolly Wolston.

The lengthy stay of the *Unicorn* at Portsmouth was due to the fact that repairs of some magnitude had become absolutely necessary after her voyage from Sydney to Europe.

Fritz and Frank did not spend the whole of this time in London or in England. They and Jenny regarded it as a duty to visit Switzerland, so as to be able to take to M. and Mme. Zermatt some news of their native land.

So they went first to France, and spent a week in Paris. The Empire had just ended at this date, as also had the long wars with

The Castaways of the Flag

Great Britain.

Fritz and Frank arrived in Switzerland, the country which they had almost forgotten, so young had they been when they left it, and from Geneva they went to the canton of Appenzel.

Of their family none remained except a few distant relatives of whom M. and Mme. Zermatt knew little. But the arrival of the two young men caused a great sensation in the Swiss Republic. Everybody knew the story of the survivors of the wreck of the *Landlord*, and knew the island now on which they had found refuge. Thus, although their fellow countrymen were little inclined to run the risks involved in emigration, several declared their intention of joining those colonists to whom New Switzerland promised a cordial welcome.

It was not without a pang that Fritz and Frank left the land of their origin. Even if they might hope to visit it again in the future, that was a hope which M. and Mme. Zermatt, advancing now in years, would hardly realize.

Crossing France, Fritz and Jenny and Frank returned to England.

Preparations for the sailing of the *Unicorn* were drawing to a close, and the corvette would be ready to set sail in the last few days of June.

Both Fritz and Frank were received with flattering attention by the Lords of the Admiralty. England was grateful to Jean Zermatt for having of his own free will offered Captain Littlestone immediate possession of his island.

As has been explained, when the corvette left New Switzerland, the greatest portion of the island was still unexplored, save the district of the Promised Land, the littoral on the north, and part of the littoral on the east as far as Unicorn Bay. Captain Littlestone was therefore to complete its survey both on the west and south and also in the interior. In a few months more, several ships would be fitted out to take emigrants and the materials required in colonization and to put the island in a proper state of defense. Then regular communication would be established between Great Britain and those distant waters of the Indian Ocean.

On the 27th of June the *Unicorn* was ready to weigh anchor, and only waited for Fritz and Jenny and Frank. On the 28th the three arrived at

Portsmouth, whither the stores purchased on behalf of the Zermatt family had been sent in advance.

They were warmly welcomed aboard the corvette by Captain Littlestone, whom they had had one or two opportunities of meeting in London. How happy they were in the thought of seeing James and Susan Wolston again at Cape Town, and also the charming little Dolly, whom Frank had kept constantly supplied with news, and good news too, of everybody.

In the morning of the 29th of June, the *Unicorn* left Portsmouth with a fair wind, flying at the peak the English flag which was to be planted upon the shores of New Switzerland.

The Castaways of the Flag

Chapter III - The Mutiny On *The Flag*

A cabin was reserved for Fritz and his wife in the *Unicorn,* and an adjoining one for Frank, and they took their meals at Captain Littlestone's table.

Nothing of special note happened during the voyage. There were all the usual incidents, changeable seas, uncertain winds, cairns, and a few violent outbreaks of heavy weather through which the corvette came without much damage. In the South Atlantic they passed a few vessels which would report tidings of the *Unicorn* in Europe. In the present interval of peace after the long period of great wars, the high seas were safe.

But the *Unicorn,* which had had a fairly easy time while crossing the Atlantic, met with shocking weather when south of Africa. A violent storm burst on her during the night of the 19th of August, and the gale drove her out to sea again. The hurricane grew more and more violent, and they had to run before it, as it was impossible to lie to. Captain Littlestone, splendidly supported by his officers and crew, displayed great skill. The mizzen mast had to be cut away, and a leak was sprung aft which was only smothered with difficulty. At last, when the wind fell, Captain Littlestone was able to resume his course and hurried to the harbor at Cape Town for repairs.

On the morning of the 10th of September the top of the Table, the mountain which gives its name to the bay, was sighted.

Directly the *Unicorn h*ad found her moorings, James Wolston, with his wife and Dolly, came out in a boat.

What a welcome they gave Fritz and Jenny and Frank, and how happy they all were!

For the last ten months they had perforce been without news. Although there was no particular ground for imagining that anything untoward had befallen the people at Rock Castle, this absence could not but seem very long.

James Wolston's affairs had all been wound up satisfactorily.

But they found themselves confronted by the impossibility of putting to sea at once. The damage done to the *Unicorn* was serious enough to necessitate a prolonged stay in Cape Town harbor. It would take two or three months to make repairs, after her cargo had been taken out of the corvette. She could not possibly sail for New Switzerland before the end of October.

But the passengers on the *Unicorn* had an unexpected opportunity of shortening their stay at the Cape.

There happened to be in the harbor a vessel, due to sail in a fortnight. She was the *Flag,* an English three-masted vessel of five hundred tons, captain Harry Gould, bound for Batavia, in the Sunday Islands. To put in at New Switzerland would take her very little out of her course, and the passengers for the island were prepared to pay a good price for their passage.

Their proposal was accepted by Captain Gould, and the *Unicorn's* passengers transferred their baggage to the *Flag.*

The three-master's preparations were finished in the afternoon of the 20th of September. That evening they said good-bye, not without regret, to Captain Littlestone, promising to look out for the arrival of the *Unicorn* at the mouth of Deliverance Bay towards the end of November.

Next morning the *Flag* sailed, with a favoring wind from the south-west, and before the evening of that first day the high summits of the Cape, left forty miles behind, disappeared below the horizon.

Harry Gould was a fine sailor, with cool courage equal to his resolution. He was now in the prime of life, at forty-two, and had shown his quality both as mate and captain.

His owners had every confidence in him.

To this confidence, Robert Borupt, the second officer on the *Flag,* was not entitled. He was a man of the same age as Harry Gould, jealous, vindictive, and of uncontrolled passions. He never believed that he received the due meed of his merits. Disappointed in his hope of being given the command of the *Flag,* he nursed at the bottom of his heart a secret hatred of his captain. But his temper had not escaped the vigilance of the boatswain, John Block, a fearless, reliable man devoted heart and soul to his chief.

The Castaways of the Flag

The crew of the *Flag*, mustering some score of men, was not of the first-class, as Captain Gould very well knew. The boatswain noticed with disapproval the indulgence too often shown by Robert Borupt to some of the sailors, when fault should have been found with them for neglect of duty. He thought that all this was suspicions, and he watched the second officer, fully determined to give Captain Gould warning, if needful.

Nothing of note happened between the 22nd of August and the 9th of September. The condition of the sea and the direction of the wind were alike favorable to the ship's progress, though the breeze was a shade too light. If the three-master were able to maintain the same rate of progress she would reach New Switzerland waters about the middle of October, within the time anticipated.

But about this time the crew began to manifest symptoms of insubordination. It even looked as though the second and third officers, in defiance of every sense of duty, connived at this relaxing of discipline. Robert Borupt, influenced by his own jealous and perverse nature, took no steps to check the disorder.

But the *Flag* continued to make her way north-east. On the 9th of September she was almost in the middle of the Indian Ocean, on the line of the Tropic of Capricorn, her position being 20° 17' latitude and 80° 45' longitude.

During the course of the previous night symptoms of bad weather had appeared-a sudden fall of the barometer, and a gathering of storm clouds, both signs of the formidable hurricanes that too often lash these seas to fury.

About three o'clock in the afternoon a squall got up so suddenly that it almost caught the ship-a serious matter for a vessel which, heeled over to one side, cannot answer to her rudder and is in danger of not being brought up again unless her rigging is cut away. If that is done, she is disabled, incapable of offering any resistance to the waves while lying to, and is at the mercy of the ocean's fury.

As soon as this storm broke the passengers had, of course, been obliged to keep their cabins, for the deck was swept by tremendous seas. Only Fritz and Frank stayed on deck to lend a hand with the crew.

Captain Gould took the watch at the outset, and the boatswain was at the wheel, while the second and third officers were on duty in the forecastle. The crew were at their posts, ready to obey the captain's orders, for it was a matter of life and death. The slightest mistake in the handling of her, while the seas were breaking over the *Flag* as she lay half over on the port side, might have meant the end.

Every effort must be made to get her up again, and then to trim her sails so as to bring her head on to the squall.

And yet the mistake was made, not deliberately perhaps, for the ship ran the risk of foundering through it, but certainly through some misunderstanding of the captain's orders, of which an officer ought not to have been capable, if he possessed any of the instincts of a sailor.

Robert Borupt, the second officer, alone was to blame. The foretopsail, trimmed at a wrong moment, drove the ship still farther over, and a tremendous lump of water crashed over the taffrail.

"That cursed Borupt wants to sink us!" cried Captain Gould.

"He has done it!" the boatswain answered, trying to shove the tiller to starboard.

The captain leaped to the deck and made his way forward at the risk of being swept back by the water. After a desperate struggle he reached the forecastle.

"Get to your cabin!" he shouted in a voice of wrath to the second officer; "get to your cabin, and stop there!"

Borupt's blunder was so patent that not one of the crew dared to protest, although they were all ready to stand by him if he had given them the word. He obeyed, however, and went back to the poop.

What was possible to do, Captain Gould did. He trimmed all the canvas that the *Flag* could carry, and succeeded in bringing her up without being obliged to cut away the rigging. The ship no longer lay broadside on to the sea.

For three consecutive days they had run before the storm in constant peril. During almost the whole of that time Susan and Jenny and Dolly were obliged to keep to their cabins, while Fritz, Frank, and James Wolston helped in the various operations.

The Castaways of the Flag

At last, on the 13th of September, an abatement of the storm came. The wind dropped, and although the sea did not immediately drop too, at last the waves no longer swept the deck of the *Flag.*

The ladies hurried eagerly out of their cabins. They knew what had taken place between the captain and the second officer, and why the latter had been removed from his post. Robert Borupt's fate would be decided by a naval court when they got back.

There was much damage to the canvas to be made good, and John Block, who was in charge of this work, saw quite clearly that the crew were on the verge of mutiny.

This state of things could not be lost upon Fritz, or Frank, or James Wolston, and it filled them with more uneasiness than the storm had caused them. Captain Gould would not shrink from the severest measures against the mutineers. But was he not too late?

During the following week there was no actual breach of discipline. As the *Flag* had been carried some hundreds of miles to the east, she had to turn back to the west, in order to get into the longitude of New Switzerland.

On the 20th of September, about ten o'clock, much to the surprise of all, for he had not been released from arrest, Robert Borupt reappeared on the deck.

The passengers, who were all sitting together on the poop, had a presentiment that the situation, grave enough already, was about to become still more grave.

Directly Captain Gould saw the second officer coming forward he went up to him.

"Mr. Borupt," he said, "you are under arrest. What are you doing here? Answer!"

"I will!" cried Borupt loudly. "And this is my answer!"

Turning to the crew, he shouted:

"Come on, mates!"

"Hurrah for Borupt!" sang from every part of the ship!

Captain Gould rushed down into his cabin and came back with a pistol in his hand. But he was not given time to use it. A shot, fired by one of the sailors round Borupt, wounded him in the head, and he fell into the boatswain's arms.

Resistance was hopeless against an entire crew of mutineers, headed by the first and second officers. John Block, Fritz, Frank, and James Wolston, drawn up near Captain Gould tried in vain to maintain the struggle. In a moment they were overwhelmed by numbers, and ten sailors hustled them down to the spardeck with the captain.

Jenny, Dolly, Susan, and the child were shut into their cabins, over which a guard was placed by order of Borupt, now ruler of the ship.

The situation of the prisoners in the semidarkness of the spar-deck, and of the wounded captain whose head could only be dressed with cold compresses, was a hard one. The boatswain was unfailing in his devotion to the captain.

Fritz and Frank and James Wolston were consumed by appalling anxiety. The three women were at the mercy of the mutineers of the *Flag!* The men suffered agony from the thought that they were powerless.

Several days passed. Twice a day, morning and evening, the hatch of the spar-deck was opened and the prisoners were given some

food. To the questions that John Block asked them, the sailors only replied with brutal threats.

More than once did the boatswain and his companions try to force up the hatch and regain their liberty. But the hatch was guarded day and night, and even if they had succeeded in raising it, overpowering their guards, and getting up on deck, what chance would they have had against the crew, and what would have been the result?

"The brute! The brute!" said Fritz over and over again, as he thought of his wife and Susan and Dolly.

"Yes; the biggest rascal alive!" John Block declared. "If he doesn't swing some day it will be because justice is dead!"

But if the mutineers were to be punished, and their ringleader given the treatment he deserved, a man-of-war must catch and seize the *Flag.*

The Castaways of the Flag

And Robert Borupt did not commit the blunder of going into waters where ships were numerous, and where he and his gang might have run the risk of being chased. He must have taken the ship far out of her proper course, most probably to the eastward, with the object of getting away alike from ships and the African and Australian shores.

Every day was adding a hundred, or a hundred and fifty, miles to the distance separating the *Flag* from the meridian of New Switzerland. Captain Gould and the boatswain could tell from the angle at which the ship heeled to port that she was making good speed. The creaking of the mast steps showed that the first officer was cramming on sail. When the *Flag* arrived in those distant waters of the Pacific Ocean where piracy was practicable, what would become of the prisoners? The mutineers would not be able to keep them; would they maroon them on some desert island? But anything would be better than to remain on board the ship, in the hands of Robert Borupt and his accomplices.

A week had passed since Harry Gould and his friends had been shut up on the spar-deck, without a word about the women. But on the 27th of September, it seemed as if the speed of the three-master had decreased, either because she was becalmed or because she was hove to.

About eight o'clock in the evening a squad of sailors came down to the captives.

These had no choice but to obey the order to follow him which the second officer gave them.

What was going on above? Was their liberty about to be restored to them? Or had a party been formed against Robert Borupt to restore Captain Gould to the command of the *Flag?*

When they were brought up on to the deck in front of all the crew, they saw Borupt waiting for them at the foot of the mainmast. Fritz and Frank cast a vain glance within the poop, the door of which was open. No lamp or lantern shed a gleam of light within.

But as they came up to the starboard nettings, the boatswain could see the top of a mast rocking against the side of the ship.

Evidently the ship's boat had been lowered to the sea.

Was Borupt preparing, then, to put the captain and his friends aboard her and cast them adrift in these waters, abandoning them to all the perils of the sea, without the least idea whether they were near any land?

And the unfortunate women, too, were they to remain on board, exposed to such appalling danger?

At the thought that they would never see them more, Fritz and Frank and James determined to make a last attempt to set them free, though it should end in dying where they stood.

Fritz rushed to the side of the poop, calling Jenny. But he was stopped, as Frank was stopped, and James was stopped before he heard any answer from Susan to his call. They were overpowered at once, and despite resistance were lowered with Captain Gould and John Block over the nettings into the ship's boat, which was fastened alongside the vessel by a knotted cable.

Their surprise and joy-yes, joy!-were inexpressible. The dear ones whom they had called in vain were in the boat already! The women had been lowered down a few minutes before the prisoners had left the spar-deck. They were waiting in mortal terror, not knowing whether their companions were to be cast adrift with them.

It seemed to them that to be reunited was the greatest grace that Heaven could have bestowed on them.

And yet what peril menaced them aboard this boat! Only four bags of biscuit and salt meat had been flung into it, with three casks of fresh water, a few cooking utensils, and a bundle of clothes and blankets taken at random from the cabins-a meagre supply at best.

But they were together! Death alone could separate them henceforward.

They were not given much time to reflect. In a few moments, with the freshening wind, the *Flag* would be several miles away.

The boatswain had taken his place at the tiller, and Fritz and Frank theirs at the foot of the mast, ready to hoist the sail directly the boat should be free from the shelter of the ship.

The Castaways of the Flag

Captain Gould had been laid down under the forward deck. Jenny was ministering to him where he lay stretched out on the blankets, for he was unable to stand.

On the *Flag* the sailors were leaning over the nettings, looking on in silence. Not one of them felt a spark of pity for their victims. Their fierce eyes gleamed in the darkness.

Just at this moment a voice was raised-the voice of Captain Gould, to whom his indignation restored some strength. He struggled to his feet, dragged himself from bench to bench, and half stood up.

"You brutes!" he cried. "You shall not escape man's justice!"

"Nor yet God's justice!" Frank added.

"Cast off!" cried Borupt.

The rope dropped into the water, the boat was left alone, and the ship disappeared into the darkness of the night.

Chapter IV - Land Ahoy!

It was Frank who had shouted "Land!" in tones of stentorian salutation. Standing erect upon the poop, he had thought he could see vague outlines of a coast through a rift in the fog. So he seized the halyards and scrambled to the masthead where, sitting astride the yard, he kept his eyes fixed steadily in the direction where he had seen it.

Close upon ten minutes passed before he caught another glimpse to the northward. He slid to the foot of the mast.

"You saw the coast?" Fritz asked sharply.

"Yes, over there; under the rim of that thick cloud which hides the horizon now."

"Are you sure you were not mistaken, Mr. Frank?" John Block said.

"No, bos'un, no, I was not mistaken! The cloud has spread over the place again now, but the land is behind it. I saw it; I swear I saw it!"

Jenny had just risen and grasped her husband's arm.

"We must believe what Frank says," she declared. "His sight is wonderfully keen. He could not make a mistake."

"I haven't made a mistake," Frank said. "You must all believe me, as Jenny does. I saw a cliff distinctly. It was visible for nearly a minute through a break in the clouds. I couldn't tell whether it ran to the east or the west; but, island or continent, the land is there!"

How could they be skeptical about what Frank declared so positively?

To what land the coast belonged they might learn when the boat had reached it. Anyhow, her passengers, five men, namely Fritz and Frank and James, Captain Gould and the boatswain John Block, and three women, Jenny, Dolly, and Susan, together with the child, would most certainly disembark upon its coast, whatever it might be.

If it offered no resources, if it were uninhabitable, or if the presence of natives made it dangerous, the boat would put to sea again, after revictualing as well as possible.

Captain Gould was immediately informed and, in spite of his weakness and pain, he insisted on being carried to the stern of the boat.

The Castaways of the Flag

Fritz began to make some comments about the signaled land.

"What is of the most concern to us at the present moment, is its distance from here. Given the height from which it was observed, and also the foggy state of the atmosphere, the distance cannot be more than twelve or fifteen miles."

Captain Gould made a sign of assent, and the boatswain nodded.

"So with a good breeze blowing towards the northward," Fritz went on, "two hours should be enough to take us to it."

"Unfortunately," said Frank, "the breeze is very uncertain, and seems to be inclined to go back. If it doesn't drop altogether I am afraid it may be against us."

"What about the oars?" Fritz rejoined.

"Can't we take to the oars, my brother and James, and I, while you take the tiller, bos'un? We could row for several hours."

"Take to the oars!" Gould commanded, in an almost inaudible voice.

It was a pity that the captain was not in a fit state to steer, for, with four of them to row, the crew might have made a better job of it.

Besides, although Fritz and Frank and James were in the full vigor of youth, and the boatswain was a sturdy fellow still, and all were thoroughly hardened to physical exercise, yet they were terribly weakened now by privation and fatigue. A week had passed since they had been cast a drift from the *Flag*. They had economized their provisions, yet only enough remained to last them for twenty-four hours. On three or four occasions they had caught a few fish by trailing lines behind the boat. A little stove, a little kettle, and a sauce pan were all the utensils they possessed, besides their pocket knives. And if this land were no more than a rocky island, if the boat were obliged to resume her painful course for more long days, looking for a continent or an island where existence might be possible-what then?

But all felt hope reviving again. Instead of the boat that was threatened by squalls and tossed about by the waves and half filled by the sea, they would at least feel firm ground under their feet. They would install themselves in some cave to shelter there from bad weather. Perhaps they would find a fertile soil, with edible roots and fruits. And there they would be able to await the passing of a ship, without need to fear hunger or thirst. The ship would see their signals, would come to the rescue of the castaways-all that and more they saw through the mirage of hope!

Did the coast thus seen belong to some group of islands situated beyond the Tropic of Capricorn? That was what the boatswain and Fritz discussed in undertones. Jenny and Dolly had resumed their seats in the bottom of the boat, and the little boy was sleeping in Mrs. Wolston's arms. Captain Gould, eaten up with fever, had been carried back under the poop, and Jenny was soaking compresses in cold water to lay upon his head.

Fritz propounded many theories, none of them very encouraging. He was pretty sure that the *Flag* had sailed a long way to the east during the week after the mutiny. In that case the boat would have been cast adrift in that part of the Indian Ocean where the charts show only a few islands, Amsterdam and Saint Paul, or, farther south, the archipelago of Kerguelen. Yet even in these islands, the former deserted, the latter inhabited, life would be assured, salvation certain, and-who could say? Some day or other they might be able to get home from there.

Besides, if since the 27th of September, the ship's boat had been carried northwards by the breeze from the south, it was just possible that this land was part of the Australian continent. If they got to Hobart Town, Melbourne, or Adelaide, they would be safe. But if the boat landed in the south-west portion, in King George's Bay or by Cape Leeuwin, a country inhabited by hordes of savages, the position would be more serious. Here at sea there was at least a chance of falling in with a ship bound for Australia or some of the Pacific Islands.

"Anyhow, Jenny," said Fritz to his wife, who had taken his place by her side again, "we must be a long way-hundreds of miles from New Switzerland."

"No doubt," Jenny answered, "but it is something that land is there! What your family did in your island, and what I did on the Burning Rock, we can do again, can't we? After being tried as we have been, we have a right to have confidence in our own energy. Two of Jean Zermatt's sons can't lose heart."

The Castaways of the Flag

"My dear wife," Fritz replied, "if ever I were to falter I should only have to listen to you! No; we will not fail, and we shall be splendidly backed up. The boatswain is a man on whom to rely utterly. As for the poor captain-"

"He will get over it, he will get well, Fritz, dear," Jenny said confidently. "The fever will drop. When we get him to land he will be better attended to, and will pick up his strength, and we shall find our leader in him once more."

"Ah, Jenny, dear," exclaimed Fritz, pressing her to his heart, "may God grant that this land can offer us the resources that we need! I don't ask for as much as we found in New Switzerland; we cannot expect that. The worst of all would be to encounter savages, against whom we have no defense, and to be obliged to put to sea again without getting fresh provisions. It would be better to land upon a desert shore even only an island. There will be fish in its waters and shells on its beaches, and perhaps flocks of birds, as we found when we got to the shore at Rock Castle. We shall contrive to revictual, and after a week or two, when we have had a rest and the captain has recovered his strength, we could set out to discover a more hospitable coast. This boat is sound and we have an excellent sailor to manage her. The rainy season is not nearly due yet. We have lived through some storms already, and we should live through more. Let this land, whatever it is, only give us some fresh provisions, and then, with the help of God-"

"Fritz, dear," Jenny answered, clasping her husband's hands in her own, "you must say all that to our companions. Let them hear you, and they will not lose heart."

"They never have, for a moment, dear wife," said Fritz; "and if they ever should falter, it is you, bravest and most capable of women, the English girl of Burning Rock, who would give them hope once more!"

All thought as Fritz did of this brave Jenny. While they had been shut up in their cabins it was from her that Dolly and Susan had been encouraged to resist despair.

One advantage this land seemed to have. It was not like New Switzerland, through whose waters merchant vessels never passed. On the contrary, whether it were the southern coast of Australia or

Tasmania, or even an island in the archipelagos of the Pacific, its position would be marked in the naval charts.

But even if Captain Gould and his companions could entertain some hope of being picked up there, they could not be otherwise than profoundly distressed by the thought of the distance that separated them from New Switzerland-hundreds of miles, no doubt, since the *Flag* had sailed steadily eastwards for a whole week.

It was now the 13th of October. Nearly a year had passed since the *Unicorn* had left the island, whither she was due to return about this time. At Rock Castle, M. and Mme. Zermatt, Ernest and Jack, Mr. and Mrs. Wolston and Hannah, were counting the days and hours.

In a few weeks more, after her stay at Cape Town, the *Unicorn* would appear in New Switzerland waters, and then the Zermatts and Wolstons would learn that their missing dear ones had taken their passage in the *Flag*, which had not been seen again. Could they doubt that she had perished with all hands in one of the frequent storms that rage in the Indian Ocean? Would there be room for hope that they would ever see her passengers again?

All that was in the future, however; the immediate present held quite enough formidable possibilities to engage their attention.

Ever since Frank had pointed out the land, the boatswain had been steadily steering in a northerly direction, not an easy task without a compass. The position indicated by Frank was only approximate, and unfortunately the thick curtain veiled the horizon line, which, from observers on the level of the sea, must still be ten or twelve miles away.

The oars had been got out. Fritz and James were rowing with all the strength they could exert. But in their state of exhaustion they could not lift the heavily loaded boat, and it would take them the entire day to cover the distance which lay between them and the shore.

God grant that the wind might not thwart all their efforts! On the whole it would be better if the calm endured till evening. Should the breeze blow from the north, the boat would be carried far back from these waters.

The Castaways of the Flag

By midday it was questionable whether more than a couple of miles had been done since morning. The boatswain suspected that a current was setting in the opposite direction.

About two o'clock in the afternoon John Block, who was standing up, exclaimed:

"A breeze is coming; I can feel it! The jib by itself will do more than the oars."

The boatswain was not mistaken. A few minutes later little flaws began to pain green the surface of the water in the south-west, and a creamy ripple spread right to the sides of the boat.

"That shows you are right, Block," said Fritz. "But still, the breeze is so faint that we must not stop rowing."

"We won't stop, Mr. Fritz," the boatswain answered; "let us plug away until the sail can carry us towards the coast."

"Where is it?" asked Fritz, trying in vain to look through the curtain of fog.

"Right in front of us, for sure!"

"Is it so certain, Block?" Frank put in.

"Where would you have it be, except behind that cursed fog up there in the north?" the boatswain retorted.

"We would have it there all right," James Wolston said. "But that is not surely enough!"

And they could not possibly know, unless the wind should freshen.

This it made no haste to do, and it was after three when the flapping of the half-clewed sail showed that it might now be of use.

The oars were taken in, and Fritz and Frank hoisted the foresail and hauled it in hard, while the boatswain secured the sheet which was thrashing the gunwale.

Was it nothing more than a capricious breeze, whose intermittent breath would not be strong enough to disperse the fog?

For twenty minutes more doubt reigned. Then the swell took the boat broadside on, and the boatswain had to bring her head round with one of the sculls. The foresail and the jib bellied out, drawing the sheets quite taut.

The direction they had to take was northward, until the wind should clear the horizon.

They hoped that this might happen as soon as the breeze had got so far. So all eyes were fixed in that direction. If the land showed only for one moment, John Block would ask no more, but would steer for it.

But no rift appeared in the veil, although went down. The boat was moving fairly fast. Fritz and the boatswain were beginning to wonder if they had passed the land.

Doubt crept into their hearts again. Had Frank been mistaken, after all? Had he really caught sight of land to the northward?

He declared again most positively that he had.

"It was a high coast," he declared a gain, "a cliff with an almost horizontal crest, and it was impossible to mistake a cloud for it."

"Yet, since we are bearing down upon it," Fritz replied, "we ought to have reached it by now. It could not have been more than twelve or fifteen miles off then."

"Are you sure, Block," Frank went on, "that you have been steering the boat on to it all the time, and that it was due north?"

"It is possible that we have got on a wrong tack," the boatswain acknowledged. "And so I think it would be better to wait until the horizon clears, even if we have to stay where we are all night."

That might be the best thing to do. But if the boat were close to the shore it would not be wise to risk it among the reefs which probably fringed it.

So all listened intently, trying to detect the least sound of surf.

Nothing was to be heard-none of the long and sullen rolling of the sea when it breaks upon reefs of rocks, or bursts in foam upon the beach.

The Castaways of the Flag

The utmost caution had to be exercised. About half-past five, the boatswain ordered the foresail to be struck. The jib was left as it was, to give steerage way.

It was the wisest thing to do, to reduce the speed of the boat until the land was sighted.

At night, in the midst of such profound darkness, there was danger in venturing near a coast-danger of counter-currents drifting on to it, though there might be no wind. In similar conditions a ship would not have delayed until the evening to put out again and seek the security of the open sea. But a boat cannot do what a ship may. To tack up against the southerly wind, which was freshening now, would have involved a risk of getting too far away-not to mention the severe toil.

So the boat stayed where it was, with only the jib sail set, hardly moving, her head pointed north.

But at last all uncertainty and all possibility of mistake was removed. About six o'clock in the evening the sun showed itself for a moment before disappearing below the waves.

On the 21st of September it set exactly in the west, and on the 13th of October, twenty-three days after the equinox, it set a little above in the southern hemisphere. Just at that moment the fog lifted, and Fritz could see the sun drawing near to the horizon. Ten minutes later its fiery disc was flush with the line of sky and sea.

"That is the north, over there!" said Fritz, pointing with his hand to a point rather to the left of that on which the boat was headed.

Almost at once he was answered by a shout, a shout that all of them uttered together.

"Land! Land!"

The mist had just dispersed, and the coast line was revealed not more than a mile away.

The boatswain steered straight for it. The foresail was set again and swelled out in the dying breeze.

Half an hour later the boat had grounded on a sandy beach, and was made fast behind a long point of rock, well sheltered from the surf.

Jules Verne

Chapter V - A Barren Shore

The castaways had reached land at last! Not one of them had succumbed to the fatigue and privations of their fortnight's voyage under such distressing and dangerous conditions, and for that thanks were due to God. Only Captain Gould was suffering terribly from fever. But in spite of his exhaustion, his life did not appear to be in danger, and a few days' rest might set him up again.

The question rose, what was this land on which they had disembarked?

Whatever it was, it unhappily was not New Switzerland, Where, but for the mutiny of Robert Borupt and his crew, the *Flag* would have arrived within the expected time. What had this unknown shore to offer instead of the comfort and prosperity of Rock Castle?

But this was not the moment to waste time over such questions. The night was so dark that nothing could be seen except a strand backed by a lofty cliff, at its sides bastions of rock. It was settled that all should remain in the boat until sunrise. Fritz and the boatswain were to keep watch until the morning. The coast might be frequented by natives, and vigilance was necessary. Whether it were Australian continent or Pacific Island, they must be upon their guard. In the event of attack they would be able to escape by putting out to sea.

Jenny, Dolly, and Susan therefore resumed their places beside Captain Gould. Frank and James stretched themselves out between the benches, ready to spring up at the call of the boatswain. But for the moment they had reached the limit of their strength, and they fell asleep immediately.

Fritz and John Block sat together in the stern and talked in low tones.

"So here we are in harbor, Mr. Fritz," said the boatswain; "I knew we should end by getting there. If it isn't, properly speaking, a harbor, you will agree at any rate that it is ever so much better than anchoring among rocks. Our boat is safe for the night. Tomorrow we will look into things."

"I envy you your cheerfulness, my dear Block," Fritz answered. "This neighborhood does not inspire me with any confidence, and our position is anything but comfortable near a coast whose bearings we do not even know."

"The coast is a coast, Mr. Fritz. It has got creeks and beaches and rocks; it is made like any other, and I don't suppose it will sink from under our feet. As for the question of leaving it, or of settling on it, we will decide that later."

"Anyhow, Block, I hope we shall not be obliged to put to sea again before the captain has had a little time to rest and recover. So if the spot is deserted, if it has resources to offer, and we run no risk of falling into the hands of natives, we must stay here some time."

"Deserted it certainly seems to be so far," the boatswain replied, "and to my thinking, it is better it should be."

"I think so, too, Block, and I think that we shall be able to renew our provisions by fishing, if we can't by hunting."

"As you say, sir. Then, if the game here only amounts to sea-birds which one can't live on, we will hunt in the forests and plains inland and make up our fishing that way. Without guns, of course."

"What brutes they were, Block, not even to leave us any firearms!"

"They were perfectly right-in their own interests, you understand," the boatswain replied. "Before we let go I could not have resisted the temptation to shoot at the head of that rascal Borupt-the treacherous hound!"

"Traitors all," Fritz added; "all of them who stood in with him."

"Well, they shall pay for their treachery some day!" John Block declared.

"Did you hear anything, bos'un?" Fritz asked suddenly, listening intently.

"No; that sound is only the ripples along the shore. There is nothing to worry about, so far, and although the night is as dark as the bottom of the hold I've got good eyes."

"Well, don't shut them for a moment, Block; let us be prepared for anything."

The Castaways of the Flag

"The hawser is ready to be cast off," the boatswain answered. "If need be, we shall only have to seize the oars, and with one shove with the boat-hook I'll guarantee to drive the boat a good twenty yards from the rocks."

More than once, however, during the night, Fritz and the boatswain were set on the alert. They thought they could hear a crawling sound upon the sandy shore.

Deep silence reigned. The breeze had died away; the sea had fallen to a calm. A slight surf breaking at the foot of the rocks was all that could be heard. A few birds, a very few, gulls and sea-mews flying in from the sea, sought their crannies in the cliffs. Nothing disturbed the first night passed upon the shore. Next morning all were astir at daybreak, and it was with sinking hearts that they examined the coast on which they had found refuge.

Fritz had been able to see part of it the day before, when it was a mile or so away. Viewed from that point it extended ten or twelve miles east and west. From the promontory at the foot of which the boat was moored, only a fifth of that, at most, could be seen, shut in between two angles with the sea beyond, clear and lucent on the right hand but still dark upon the left. The shore extended for a stretch of perhaps a mile, enclosed at each end by lofty bastions of rock, while a black cliff completely shut it in behind.

This cliff must have been eight or nine hundred feet in height, rising sheer from the beach, which sloped steeply up to its base. Was it higher still beyond? That could only be ascertained by scaling the crest by means of the bastions, one of which, the one to the east, running rather farther out to sea, presented an outline that was not so perpendicular. Even on that side, however, the ascent would be an uncommonly difficult one, if indeed it were not impracticable.

Captain Gould and his companions were first conscious of a feeling of utter discouragement as they beheld the wild desolation of this carpet of sand, with points of rock jutting out here and there. Not a tree, not a bush, not a trace of vegetation! Here were the melancholy and horror of the desert. The only verdure was that of scanty lichens, those rudimentary productions of nature, rootless, stalkless, leafless, flowerless, looking like scabby patches on the sides of the rocks, and of every tint from faded yellow to brilliant red. In some places, too, there

45

was a kind of sticky mildew caused by the damp. At the edge of the cliff there was not a blade of grass; on its granite wall there was not a single one of those stone-crops or rock plants which need so very little soil.

Was it to be deduced that soil was lacking on the plateau above as well? Had the boat found nothing better than one of those desert islands undeserving of a name?

"It certainly isn't what you might call a gay place," the boatswain murmured in Fritz's ear.

"Perhaps we should have had better luck if we had come ashore on the west or east."

"Perhaps," Block assented; "but at any rate we shall not run up against any savages here."

For it was obvious that not even a savage could have existed on this barren shore.

Jenny, Frank, Dolly, James, and Susan sat in the boat, surveying the whole coast, so different from the verdant shores of the Promised Land. Even Burning Rock, gloomy of aspect as it was, had had its natural products to offer to Jenny Montrose, the fresh water of its stream and the game in its woods and plains. Here was nothing but stones and sand, a bank of shells on the left, and long trails of sea-weeds left high and dry by the tide. Verily, a land of desolation!

The animal kingdom was represented by a few sea-birds, gulls, black-divers, sea-mews, and swallows, which uttered deafening cries at finding their solitude disturbed by the presence of man. Higher up, great frigate-birds, halcyons and albatrosses sailed on powerful wings.

"Well," said the boatswain at last, "even if this shore is not so good as yours in New Switzerland, that's no reason for not landing on it."

"Then let us land," Fritz answered. "I hope we shall find somewhere to shelter at the foot of the cliff."

"Yes, let us land," said Jenny.

"Dear wife," said Fritz, "I advise you to remain here in the boat, with Mrs. Wolston and Dolly, while we make our trip. There is no sign of danger, and you have nothing to be afraid of."

"Besides," the boatswain added, "we most likely shan't go out of sight."

Fritz jumped on to the sand, followed by the others, while Dolly called out cheerfully:

"Try to bring us back something for dinner, Frank! We are relying upon you."

"We must rely upon you rather, Dolly," Frank replied. "Put out some lines at the foot of those rocks."

"We had better not land," Mrs. Wolston agreed. "We will do our best while you are away."

"The great thing," Fritz remarked, "is to keep what little biscuit we have left, in case we are obliged to put to sea again."

"Now, Mrs. Fritz," John Block said, "get the stove going. We are not the kind of people to be satisfied with lichen soup or boiled pebbles, and we promise to bring you something solid and substantial."

The weather was fairly fine. Through the clouds in the east a few sun-rays filtered.

Fritz, Frank, James, and the boatswain trudged together along the edge of the shore, over sand still wet from the last high tide.

Ten feet or so higher the sea-weeds lay in zig-zag lines.

Some were of kinds which contain nutritive substances, and John Block exclaimed:

"Why, people eat that-when they haven't got anything else! In my country, in Irish sea-ports, a sort of jam is made of that!"

After walking three or four hundred yards in this direction, Fritz and his companions came to the foot of the bastion to the west. Formed of enormous rocks with slippery surfaces, and almost perpendicular, it plunged straight down into the clear and limpid water which the slight

47

surf scarcely disturbed. Its foundations could be seen seven or eight fathoms below.

To climb along this bastion was quite impossible for it rose perpendicularly. It would be necessary to scale the cliff in order to find out if the upper plateau displayed a less arid surface. Moreover, if they had to abandon the idea of climbing this bastion it meant that they could only get round it by means of the boat. The matter of present urgency, however, was to look for some cavity in the cliff wherein they could take shelter.

So all went up to the top of the beach, along the base of the bastion.

When they reached the corner of the cliff, they came upon thick layers of sea-weeds, absolutely dry. As the last water-marks of the high tide were visible more than two hundred yards lower down, this meant-the steep pitch of the shore being taken into account-that these plants had been thrown up so far, not by the sea, but by the winds from the south, which are very violent in these waters.

"If we were obliged to spend the winter here," Fritz remarked, "these sea-weeds would supply us with fuel for a long time, if we could not find any wood."

"Fuel that burns fast," the boatswain added. "Before we came to the end of heaps like that, of course. But we have still got something to boil the pot with today. Now we must find something to put in it!"

"Let's look about," Frank answered.

The cliff was formed by irregular strata. It was easy to recognize the crystalline nature of these rocks, where feldspar and gneiss were mixed, an enormous mass of granite, of plutonic origin and extreme hardness.

This formation recalled in no respect to Fritz and Frank the walls of their own island from Deliverance Bay to False Hope Point, where limestone only was found, easily broken by pick or hammer. It was thus that the grotto of Rock Castle had been fashioned. Out of solid granite, any such work would have been impossible.

Fortunately there was no need to make any such attempt. A hundred yards from the bastion, behind the piles of sea-wrack, they found a number of openings in the rock. They resembled the cells of a gigantic hive, and possibly gave access to the inside of the rock.

The Castaways of the Flag

There were indeed several cavities at the foot of this cliff.

While some provided only small recesses, others were deep and also dark, owing to the heaps of sea-weed in front of them. But it was quite likely that in the opposite part, which was less exposed to the winds from the sea, some cavern opened into which they might carry the stores from the boat.

Trying to keep as near as possible to where the boat was moored, Fritz and his companions walked towards the eastern bastion. They hoped to find this more practicable than the other, because of its elongated outline in its lower portion, and thought that they might be able to get round it. Although it stood up sheer in its upper portion, it sloped towards the middle and ended in a point by the sea.

Their anticipations were not disappointed. In the corner formed by the bastion was a cave quite easy of access. Sheltered from the easterly, northerly, and southerly winds, its position exposed it only to the winds from the west, less frequent in these regions.

The four men went inside this cave, which was light enough for them to see all over it. It was some twelve feet high, twenty feet wide, and fifty or sixty feet deep, and contained several unequal recesses forming, as it were, so many rooms set round a common hall. It had a carpet of fine sand, free from any trace of damp. Entrance to it was through a mouth which could be easily closed.

"As I am a boatswain," John Block declared, "we couldn't have found anything better!"

"I agree," Fritz replied. "But what worries me is that this beach is absolute desert, and I am afraid the upper plateau may be so too."

"Let us begin by taking possession of the cave, and we will attend to the rest presently."

"Oh!" said Frank. "That is not much like our house at Rock Castle, and I don't even see a stream of fresh water to take the place of our Jackal River!"

"Patience! Patience!" the boatswain answered. "We shall find some spring all right by and by among the rocks, or else a stream coming down from the top of the cliff."

"Anyhow," Fritz declared, "we must not think of settling on this coast. If we do not succeed in getting round the base of those bastions on foot we must take the boat and reconnoitre beyond them. If it is a small island we have come ashore upon, we will only stay long enough to set Captain Gould up again. A fortnight will be enough, I imagine."

"Well, we have the house, at all events," John Block remarked. "As for the garden, who is to say that it isn't quite close by-on the other side of this point, perhaps?"

They left the cave and walked down across the beach, so as to get round the bastion. From the cave to the first rocks washed by the sea at the half-ebb was about two hundred yards. On this side there were none of the heaps of sea-weeds found on the left-hand side of the beach. This promontory was formed of heavy masses of rocks which seemed to have been broken off from the top of the cliff. At the cave it would have been impossible to cross it, but nearer the sea it was low enough to get across.

The boatswain's attention was soon caught by a sound of running water.

A hundred feet from the cave, a stream murmured among the rocks, escaping in little liquid threads.

The stones were scattered here, which enabled them to reach the bed of a little stream fed by a cascade that came leaping down to lose itself in the sea.

"There it is! There it is! Good fresh water!" John Block exclaimed, after a draught taken up in his hands.

"Fresh and sweet!" Frank declared when he had moistened his lips with it.

"And why shouldn't there be vegetation on the top of the cliff," John Block enquired, "although that is only a stream?"

"A stream now," Fritz said, "and a stream which may even dry up during the very hot weather, but no doubt a torrent in the rainy season."

"Well, if it will only flow for a few days longer," the boatswain remarked philosophically, "we won't ask anything more of it."

The Castaways of the Flag

Fritz and his companions now had a cave in which to establish their quarters, and a stream which would enable them to refill the boat's casks with fresh water. The chief remaining question was whether they could provide themselves with food.

Things did not look too promising. After crossing the little river the explorers had a fresh and deep disappointment.

Beyond the promontory a creek was cut into the coast, in width about half a mile, fringed with a rim of sand, and enclosed behind by the cliff. At the far end rose a perpendicular bluff, whose foot was washed by the sea.

This shore presented the same arid appearance as the other. Here, too, the vegetable growths were confined to patches of lichen and layers of sea-weeds thrown up by the tide. Was it, then, on a mere islet, a rocky, lonely, uninhabitable island in the Pacific Ocean, that the boat had come ashore? There seemed every reason to fear so.

It appeared useless to carry the exploration as far as the bluff which enclosed the creek. They were about to go back to the boat when James stretched out his hand towards the shore and said:

"What is that I see down there on the sand? Look-those moving specks. They look like rats."

From the distance it did, indeed, look as if a number of rats were on march together towards the sea.

"Rats?" said Frank enquiringly. "The rat is game, when he belongs to the *ondatra* genus.

Do you remember the hundreds we killed, Fritz, when we made that trip after the boa constrictor?"

"I should think I do, Frank," Fritz answered; "and I remember, too, that we did not make much of a feast off their flesh, which reeked too much of the marsh."

"Right!" said the boatswain. "Properly cooked, one can eat those beggars. But there's no occasion to argue about it. Those black specks over there aren't rats."

"What do you think they are, Block?" Fritz asked.

"Turtles."

"I hope you are right."

The boatswain's good eyesight might have been trusted. There actually was a crowd of turtles crawling over the sand.

So while Fritz and James remained on watch on the promontory, John Block and Frank slid down the other side of the rocks, in order to cut off the band of chelones.

These tortoises were small, measuring only twelve or fifteen inches, and long in the tail. They belonged to a species whose principal food consists of insects. There were fifty of them, on march, not towards the sea, but towards the mouth of the stream, where a quantity of sticky laminariae, left by the ebb tide, were soaking.

On this side the ground was studded with little swellings, like bubbles in the sand, the meaning of which Frank recognized at once.

"There are turtles' eggs under those!" he exclaimed.

"Well, dig up the eggs, Mr. Frank," John Block replied. "I'll belay the fowls! That's certainly ever so much better than my boiled pebbles, and if little Miss Dolly isn't satisfied-"

"The eggs will be warmly welcomed, Block, you may be sure," Frank declared.

"And the turtles, too; they are excellent beasts-excellent for making soup, I mean!"

A moment later the boatswain and Frank had turned a score of them over on to their backs. They were quite helpless in that position. Laden with half a dozen of them, and twice as many eggs, they went back towards the boat.

Captain Gould listened eagerly to John Block's story. Since he had been spared the shaking of the boat his wound had been paining him less, the fever was beginning to go down, and a week's rest would certainly put him on his feet again. Wounds in the head, unless they are exceptionally serious, generally heal easily and soon. The bullet had only grazed the surface of the skull, after tearing away part of the cheek; but it had been within an ace of going through the temple. A speedy improvement could now be looked for in the condition of the wounded man, thanks to the rest and care which he could now obtain.

It was with much satisfaction Captain Gould learned that turtles abounded in this bay, which was named Turtle Bay in their honor. It meant the guarantee of a wholesome and plentiful food, even for a considerable time. It might even be possible to preserve some of it in salt and load the boat with it when the time came to put to sea again.

For of course they would have later to seek a more hospitable shore to the northward, if the table-land at the top of the cliff proved to be as infertile as that of Turtle Bay, if it had no woods or grass lands, if, in short, the land on which the passengers of the *Flag* had come ashore proved to be nothing more than a mere heap of rocks.

"Well, Dolly, and you, too, Jenny," said Frank when he got back, "are you satisfied? How has the fishing gone while we have been away?"

"Pretty well," Jenny answered, pointing to several fish lying on the poop.

"And we've got something better than that to offer you," added Dolly, merrily.

"What's that, then?" Fritz asked.

"Mussels," the girl answered. "There are heaps of them at the foot of the promontory. Look at those boiling in the saucepan now!"

"Congratulations!" said Frank. "And you owe us congratulations, too, Jenny, for we have not come back empty-handed. Here are some eggs."

"Hens' eggs?" Bob exclaimed eagerly.

"No; turtles'," Frank replied.

"Turtles' eggs?" Jenny repeated. "Did you find turtles?"

"A regiment of them," the boatswain told her; "and there are lots more; there are enough to last us all the time we shall be at anchor in the bay."

"Before we leave this bay," Captain Gould put in, "I think we ought to reconnoitre along the coast, or climb to the top of the cliff."

"We'll try it, captain," John Block answered.

"But don't let's be in a greater hurry than we need be, since it is possible to exist here without touching what we have left of the biscuit."

"That's what I think, Block."

"What we want, captain," Frank went on, "is that you should have a rest to allow your wound to heal, and you to get back your strength. A week or two is nothing to spend here. When you are on your feet again you will have a look at things for yourself, and you will decide what is best to be done."

During the morning they proceeded to unload the boat of all that it contained, the bag of biscuit, the casks, the fuel, the utensils, and the clothing, and everything was carried within the cave. The little stove was set up in the corner of the bastion, and was first employed in making the turtle soup.

As for Captain Gould, he was carried to the cave by Fritz and the boatswain; a comfortable bed was waiting ready for him, made of dry sea-weed by Jenny and Dolly, and there he was able to enjoy several hours' sleep.

The Castaways of the Flag

Chapter VI - Time Of Trial

It would have been difficult to find better quarters than those provided by this cave. The various recesses hollowed out inside it made capital separate rooms.

It was a trifling disadvantage, that these recesses, which were of varying depth, were rather dark during the day, and that the cave itself was never very light. For, except in bad weather, it would only be occupied at night. At earliest dawn Captain Gould would be carried outside, to drink in the salt, invigorating air and bask in the sunshine.

Inside the cave Jenny arranged to occupy one of the recesses with her husband. A larger one, sufficient to accommodate all three of them, was taken possession of by James Wolston and his wife and little Bob. Frank contented himself with a corner in the large hall, where he shared the company of the skipper and the boatswain.

The remainder of the day was given up entirely to rest. The boat's passengers had to recuperate after the many emotions of this last week and the awful trial they had endured so bravely.

Wisdom dictated their resolution to spend a fortnight in this bay, where material existence seemed to be secured for some time to come. Even if the Captain's condition had not required that they should do so, John Block would not have advised an immediate departure.

In the evening, after a second meal of turtle soup, and turtle flesh and eggs, Frank led them in prayer, and all went into the cave. Captain Gould, thanks to the ministrations of Jenny and Dolly, was no longer shaking with fever. His wound now closing, gave him less pain. He was progressing rapidly towards complete recovery.

To keep a watch during the night was needless. There was nothing to fear on this lonely shore, neither savages nor wild beasts. It was unlikely that these gloomy and depressing wastes had ever been visited by man before. The stillness was only broken by the harsh and melancholy cry of the sea-birds as they came home to their crannies in the cliff. The breeze died gradually away, and not a breath of air stirred till the rising of the sun.

The men were out at daybreak. First of all John Block went down the beach along the promontory and made for the boat. It was still floating but would soon be left high and dry by the ebb tide. Being fastened by hawsers on both sides, it had not bumped against the rocks, even when the tide was at its highest, and as long as the wind continued to blow from the east it could come to no harm. In the event of the wind veering to the south they would see if it was necessary to look for other moorings. Meantime the weather seemed to be definitely set fair, and this was the fine season.

When he got back the boatswain sought out Fritz and spoke to him about this.

"It's worth giving a little thought to," he said. "Our boat comes before everything else. A snug cave is fine. But one doesn't go to sea in a cave, and when the time comes for us to leave-if it ever does come-it's important that we shouldn't be prevented from doing so."

"Of course, Block," Fritz answered. "We will take every possible care to prevent the boat coming to harm. Do you think perhaps there is a better mooring for her on the other side of the promontory?"

"We'll see, sir, and since everything is all right on this side I will go round to the other and hunt turtles. Will you come with me?"

"No, Block. Go alone. I am going back to the captain. This last good night's rest must have reduced the fever. When he wakes he will want to discuss the situation. I must be there to tell him all that has happened."

"Quite right, Mr. Fritz; and mind you tell him that there is nothing to be uneasy about at present."

The boatswain went to the far end of the promontory, and sprang from rock to rock across the creek towards the place where he and Frank had come upon the turtles the day before.

Fritz returned to the cave, up to which Frank and James were busy bringing armfuls of sea-weed. Mrs. Wolston was dressing little Bob. Jenny and Dolly were still with the captain. In the corner of the promontory the fire crackled under the stove, and the kettle began to boil, white steam escaping from its spout.

The Castaways of the Flag

When Fritz had finished his conversation with the captain, he and Jenny went down to the beach. They walked a little way and then turned back under the lofty cliff which enclosed them like a prison wall.

Fritz spoke in tones of deep emotion.

"Dear wife, I must talk to you of what is in my heart. I can see you with me in the canoe after I had found you upon Burning Rock. And then our meeting with the pinnace, and our return to Rock Castle with all the others! Two happy years slipped by with nothing to mar their quiet happiness! You were the joy and charm of our circle. We were so accustomed to life under those conditions that it seemed as if there were no world outside our island. And if it had not been for the thought of your father, beloved, perhaps we should not have sailed on the *Unicorn*-perhaps we should never have left New Switzerland."

"Why do you talk now of this, Fritz, dear?" said Jenny, greatly moved.

"I want to tell you how heavy my heart has been since ill fortune has set in upon us. Yes! I am full of remorse at having brought you to share it with me!"

"You must not fear ill fortune," Jenny answered. "A man of your courage, your energy, will not give way to despair, Fritz."

"Let me finish, Jenny! One day the *Unicorn* arrived, over there, off New Switzerland. She went away again, and took us to Europe. From that moment misfortune has never ceased to strike you. Colonel Montrose died before he could see his child-"

"Poor father!" said Jenny, her eyes wet. "Yes, that happiness was withheld from him of clasping me in his arms, and rewarding my rescuer by placing my hand in his. But God willed otherwise, and we must submit."

"Well, Jenny dear," Fritz went on, "at all events there you were, back in England; you had seen your own land again; you might have remained there with your own people and found quiet happiness."

"Happiness! Without you, Fritz?"

"And then, Jenny, you would not have incurred fresh dangers, after all those which you had escaped so miraculously. Yet you consented to follow me back to our island again."

"Do you forget that I am your wife, Fritz? Could I have hesitated to leave Europe, to rejoin all those whom I love, your family, which is mine henceforward?"

"But Jenny, Jenny, that does not make it less true that I drew you into fresh danger and danger that I cannot think of without panic. Our present situation is desperate. Oh! those mutineers who caused it all, who cast us adrift! And you, shipwrecked once in the *Dorcas,* now cast again upon an unknown island even less habitable than Burning Rock!"

"But I am not alone; I have you, and Frank, and our friends, brave and determined men. Fritz, I shrink from no dangers present or to come! I know that you will do everything possible for our safety."

"Everything, my darling," Fritz exclaimed, "but though the thought that you are there must double my courage, yet it also grieves me so much that I want to throw myself at your knees and beg for your forgiveness! It is my fault that-"

"Fritz," she answered, clinging to him, "no one could possibly have foreseen the things which have happened-the mutiny, and our being cast adrift at sea. Far better forget the ill fortune and contemplate only the good! We might have been murdered by the crew of the *Flag,* or doomed to the tortures of hunger and thirst in the boat. We might have perished in some storm. But instead we have reached a land which is not quite without resources, which at least gives us shelter. If we do not know what land it is we must try to find out, and we will leave it if we find that we must."

"To go-whither, my poor Jenny"

"Somewhere else, as our dear boatswain would say; to go wherever God wills that we shall!"

"My dear wife! Fritz exclaimed. "You have given me back my courage! Yes! We will fight on; we will not give way to despair. We will think of the precious lives that are confided to our care. We will save them! We will save them-with the help of God!"

The Castaways of the Flag

"On whom we never call in vain!" said Frank, who had overheard the last words spoken by his brother. "Let us keep our trust in Him, and He will not forsake us!"

Under Jenny's encouragement Fritz recovered all his energy. His companions were as ready as he was to spend themselves in superhuman efforts.

About ten o'clock, as the weather was fine, Captain Gould was able to come and stretch himself in the sun at the far end of the promontory. The boatswain returned from his trip round the creek as far as the foot of the bluff to the east. Beyond that it was impossible to go. Even at low tide it would have been useless to attempt to get round the foot of this huge rock, about which the surf beat violently.

John Block had been joined by James in the creek, and both brought back turtles and eggs. These chelones swarmed upon the shore. In anticipation of an early departure it would be possible to lay in a large stock of their flesh, which would secure a supply of food for the passengers.

After luncheon the men talked while Jenny, Polly, and Susan busied themselves washing the spare linen in the fresh water of the stream. It would dry quickly in the sun, for the day was hot. Afterward, all the clothes were to be mended, so that everybody might be ready to go aboard the boat again directly it should be decided to make a start.

They had important questions to answer. What was the geographical position of this land? Was it possible to ascertain it without instruments, within a few degrees, taking the position of the sun at noon as a basis for calculation? Such an observation could not be absolutely accurate. But today it seemed to confirm the opinion, already advanced by Captain Gould, that this land must lie between the fortieth and thirtieth parallels. What meridian crossed it from north to south there were no means of ascertaining, although the *Flag* must have been somewhere in the western waters of the Pacific Ocean.

Then the idea of reaching the upper plateau came up again. Pending the recovery of the captain, was it not necessary to find out whether the boat had come ashore on a continent, an island, or a mere islet? As the cliff was seven or eight hundred feet high it was quite possible that some other land might be visible a few miles out at sea. So Fritz and

Frank and the boatswain made up their minds to climb to the top of the cliff.

Several days passed without bringing any change in the situation. Every one realized the necessity of escaping from it somehow or other, and all were seriously afraid that it might become worse. The weather remained fine. The heat was great, but there was no thunder.

On several occasions John Block and Fritz and Frank had walked round the bay from the western bastion as far as the bluff. In vain had they looked for a gorge or less precipitous slope by which they might gain the plateau above. The wall rose sheer.

Meantime the captain approached complete recovery. His wound was healed, though it was still bandaged. The attacks of fever had become more and more rare, and had now ceased. His strength was coming back slowly, but he could now walk unsupported. He was always talking to Fritz and the boatswain of the chances of another voyage in the boat northward. On the morning of the 25th, he was able to go as far as the foot of the bluff, and agreed that it was impossible to walk round the base of it.

Fritz, who had accompanied him, with Frank and John Block, offered to dive into the sea and so get to the shore beyond. But although he was an excellent swimmer, there was such a current running at the foot of the bluff that the captain was obliged to order the young man not to put this dangerous idea into execution. Once borne away by the current, who could say if Fritz could have got back to the shore?

"No," said Captain Gould, "it would be rash, and there is no good in running into danger. We will go in the boat to reconnoitre that part of the coast, and if we go a few cables' length out, we shall be able to get a more extended view of it. Unfortunately I am very much afraid that it will be found to be as barren everywhere as it is here."

"You mean that we are on some islet?" Frank remarked.

"There is reason to suppose so," the captain replied.

"Very well," said Fritz, "but does it follow that this islet is an isolated point? Why should it not be part of some group of islands lying to the north, east, or west?"

"What group, my dear Fritz?" the captain retorted. "If, as everything goes to show, we are in Australian or New Zealand waters here, there is no group of islands in this part of the Pacific."

"Because the charts don't show any, does it follow that there aren't any?" Fritz remarked.

"The position of New Switzerland was not known and yet-"

"Quite true," Harry Gould replied; "that was because it lies outside the track of shipping. Very seldom, practically never, do ships cross that bit of the Indian Ocean where it is situated, whereas to the south of Australia the seas are very busy, and no island, or group of any size, could possibly have escaped the notice of navigators."

"There is still the possibility that we are somewhere near Australia," Frank went on.

"A distinct possibility," the captain answered, "and I should not be surprised if we are at its south-west extremity, somewhere near Cape Leeuwin. In that case we should have to fear the ferocious Australian natives."

"And so," the boatswain remarked, "it is better to be on an islet, where at any rate one is sure not to run up against cannibals."

"And that is what we should probably know if we could get to the top of the cliff," Frank added.

"Yes," said Fritz; "but there isn't a single place where we can do it."

"Not even by climbing up the promontory?" Captain Gould asked.

"It is practicable, although very difficult, as far as half way," Fritz answered, "but the upper walls are absolutely perpendicular. We should have to use ladders, and even then success isn't certain. If there were some chimney which we could get up with ropes, it might perhaps be possible to reach the top, but there isn't one anywhere."

"Then we will take the boat and reconnoitre the coast," said Captain Gould.

"When you are completely recovered, captain, and not before," replied Fritz firmly.

"It will be several days yet before-"

"I am getting better, Fritz," the captain declared; "how could it be otherwise, with all the attention I have? Mrs. Wolston and your wife and Dolly would have cured me merely by looking at me. We will put to sea in forty-eight hours at least."

"Westward or eastward?" Fritz asked.

"According to the wind," the captain replied.

"And I have an idea that this trip will be a lucky one," the boatswain put in.

Fritz, Frank, and John Block had already done all but the impossible in their attempts to scale the promontory. They had got about two hundred feet up, although the gradient was very steep, by slipping from one rock to the next in the very middle of a torrent of landslides, with the agility of chamois or ibex; but a third of the way up they had come to a stop. It had been a highly dangerous attempt, and the boatswain had come within an ace of breaking some of his bones.

But from that point all their attempts to continue the ascent were in vain. The promontory ended here in a vertical section with a smooth surface. There was not a foothold anywhere, not the tiniest projection on which the boat's ropes might have been caught. And they were still six or seven hundred feet from the top of the cliff.

When they returned to the cave Captain Gould explained the decision which had been reached. Two days hence, on the 27th of October, the boat was to leave her moorings to go along the coast. Had a trip of several days' duration been involved, everybody would have gone in the boat. But as only a general reconnaissance was contemplated, he thought it would be better that only he should go with Fritz and the boatswain. They three would be enough to handle the boat, and they would not go farther away to the north than they must. If they found that the coast-line bounded nothing more than an islet they could make the circuit of it and be back within twenty-four hours.

Short as their absence might be, the idea of it excited great uneasiness. The rest of the party would not be able to see their companions go without much anxiety. How could they tell what might happen? Suppose they were attacked by savages-suppose they could not get back soon-suppose they did not come back at all?

Jenny used these arguments with characteristic energy. She insisted that the many anxieties they endured already should not be added to by others arising from an absence which might be prolonged. Fritz sympathized with her arguments, Captain Gould accepted them, and ultimately it was agreed that they should all take part in the projected exploration.

As soon as this decision had been arrived at, to the general satisfaction, John Block got busy putting the boat in order. Not that it required any repairs, for it had come to little harm since it had been cast adrift, but it was well to overhaul it and fit it up in anticipation of a possible extension of the voyage to some adjoining land. So the boatswain worked his hardest to make it more comfortable, enclosing the fore-deck so that the women might have shelter from squalls and breaking waves.

There was nothing more to do but wait, and meanwhile lay in provisions for a voyage which might perhaps be longer than was intended. Besides, if it were necessary to leave Turtle Bay finally, ordinary prudence suggested that they should do so without delay, that they should take advantage of the fine season just beginning in these southern regions.

They could not but quail before the idea of a winter here. True, the cave offered them a sure shelter against the storms from the south, which are appalling in the Pacific. The cold, too, could no doubt be faced, for there would be no lack of fuel, thanks to the enormous collection of sea-weed at the foot of the cliff.

But suppose the turtles failed? Would they be reduced to fish as sole diet? And the boat-where could they put that in safety, out of reach of the waves which must break right up to the back of the beach in the winter? Would they be able to haul it up above the highest tide-marks? Harry Gould and Fritz and the rest had only their own arms to rely on, not a tool, not a lever, not a lifting-jack, and the boat was heavy enough to resist their united efforts.

At this time of year there was happily nothing but passing storms to fear. The fortnight that they had spent ashore had enabled them all to pick up their moral and physical strength as well as to recover confidence.

Their preparations were completed in the morning of the 26th. Fritz observed with some uneasiness that clouds were beginning to gather in the south. They were still a long way off, but were assuming a lurid hue. The breeze was almost imperceptible, yet the heavy mass of cloud was rising in a solid body. If this thunderstorm burst it would burst full upon Turtle Bay.

Hitherto the rocks at the far end of the promontory had protected the boat from the easterly winds. From the other side, too, the westerly winds could not have touched it, and firmly held as it was by hawsers, it might have escaped too severe a buffeting. But if a furious sea swept in from the open main, it would be unprotected and might be smashed to pieces. It was useless to think of trying to find some other mooring on the other side of the bluff or of the bastion, for, even in calm weather, the sea broke there with violence.

"What's to be done?" Fritz asked the boatswain, and the boatswain had no answer.

One hope remained-that the storm might blow itself out before it fell upon the coast. But as they listened they could hear a distant rumbling, although the wind was very faint. The sea was roaring out there in the distance, and already intermittent flaws were sweeping over its surface, giving it a livid tint.

Captain Gould gazed at the horizon.

"We are in for a bad spell," Fritz said to him.

"I am afraid we are," the captain acknowledged; "as bad a spell as our worst fears could have imagined!"

"Captain," the boatswain broke in, "this isn't a time to sit and twiddle one's thumbs. We've got to use a little elbow grease, as sailormen say."

"Let us try to pull the boat up to the top of the beach," said Fritz, calling James and his brother.

"We will try," Captain Gould replied.

The Castaways of the Flag

"The tide is coming up and will help us. Meanwhile let us begin by lightening the boat as much as we can."

All buckled to. The sails were laid upon the sand, the mast unstepped, the rudder unshipped, and the seats and spars were taken out and carried within the cave. By the time the tide was slack the boat had been hauled about twenty yards higher up. But that was not enough; she would have to be pulled up twice as far again to be out of reach of the waves.

Having no other tools, the boatswain pushed planks under the keel, and all combined to pull and push. But their efforts were useless: the heavy boat was fixed in the sand and did not gain an inch beyond the last high-water mark.

When evening came the wind threatened a hurricane. From the piled clouds in the zenith flash after flash of lightning broke, followed by terrific peals of thunder, which the cliff reechoed in appalling reverberations.

Although the boat had been left high and dry by the ebb tide, the waves, momentarily becoming stronger, would soon lift it up from the stern.

And now the rain fell in big drops, so heavily charged with electricity that they seemed to explode as they struck the sand on the shore.

"You can't stay outside any longer, Jenny, dear," said Fritz. "Do go back into the cave, I beg you! You, too, Dolly, and you too, Mrs. Wolston."

Jenny did not want to leave her husband. But Captain Gould spoke authoritatively.

"Go inside, Mrs. Fritz," he said.

"You too, captain," she replied; "you must not expose yourself to a wetting yet."

"I have nothing to fear now," Harry Gould answered.

"Jenny, I tell you again, go back, there's no time to lose!" Fritz exclaimed.

And Jenny, Dolly, and Susan took refuge in the cave just as the rain, in which hail was mingled, began to rattle down like grapeshot.

Captain Gould and the boatswain, Fritz, Frank, and James remained near the boat, though it was with the utmost difficulty that they stood up against the squalls which swept the shore. The waves were breaking in the bay already and throwing their spray right over it.

The danger was acute. Would it be possible to sustain the boat against the shocks which were rolling it from one side to the other? If it were broken up, how would Captain Gould and his companions be able to get away from this coast before the winter?

All five stood by, and when the sea came farther up and lifted the boat, they hung on to its sides trying to steady it.

Soon the storm was at its height. From twenty places at once tremendous flashes of lightning burst. When they struck the bastions they tore off fragments which could be heard crashing upon the heaps of sea-weed.

An enormous wave, twenty-five or thirty feet high at least, was lifted up by the hurricane and dashed upon the shore like a huge waterspout.

Caught in its grip Captain Gould and his companions were swept right up to the heaps of sea-weed, and it was only by a miracle that the enormous wave did not carry them back with it as it drew again to the sea!

The disaster feared so much had befallen them! The boat, torn from its bed, swept up to the top of the beach and then carried down again to the rocks at the end of the promontory, was smashed, and its fragments, after floating for a moment in the creaming foam of the backwater, disappeared from view round the bend of the bluff!

Chapter VII - The Coming Of The Albatross

The situation seemed worse than ever. While they were in the boat, exposed to all the perils of the sea, Captain Gould and his passengers at least had a chance of being picked up by some ship, or of reaching land. They had not fallen in with a ship. And although they had reached land, it was practically uninhabitable, yet it seemed they must give up all hope of ever leaving it.

"Still," said John Block to Fritz, "if we had run into a storm like that out at sea, our boat would have gone to the bottom and taken us with it!"

Fritz made no reply. He hurried through a deluge of rain and hail to take shelter with Jenny and Dolly and Susan, who were intensely anxious. Owing to its position in the corner of the promontory, the inside of the cave had not been flooded.

Towards midnight, when the rain had stopped, the boatswain piled a heap of seaweed near the mouth of the cave. A bright fire soon blazed, drying their drenched clothes.

Until the fury of the storm abated the whole sky was incessantly a blaze. The pealing thunder diminished as the clouds were driven rapidly towards the north. But as long as distant lightning continued to light up the bay, the wind blew with great force, lifting billows which plunged and broke wildly on the shore.

At dawn the men came out of the cave. Tattered clouds were passing over the cliff. Some, hanging lower, skimmed the surface. During the night the lightning had struck it in several places. Huge fragments of rock lay at its base. But there was no sign of a new cleft or crevice into which it might be possible to squeeze, and so to reach the plateau above.

Captain Gould, Fritz, and John Block took stock of what was left of the boat. It comprised the mast, the foresail and the jib, the rigging, the hawsers, the rudder, the oars, the anchor and its cable, the wooden seats, and the casks of fresh water. Some use could no doubt be made of most of these things, damaged as they were.

"Fortune has tried us cruelly!" Fritz said. "If only we had not these poor women with us, three women and a child! What fate awaits them here on this shore, which we cannot even leave now!"

Even Frank, with all his faith, kept silence this time. What could he say?

But John Block was wondering whether the storm had not brought yet another disaster upon the shipwrecked company, for so they might well be described. Was there not good reason to fear that the turtles might have been destroyed by the breakers, and their eggs smashed as the sand was washed away? It would be an irreparable loss if this food supply failed.

The boatswain made a sign to Frank to come to him, and said a few words in an undertone. Then both crossed the promontory and went down to the creek, intending to go over it as far as the bluff.

While Captain Gould, Fritz, and James went towards the western bastion, Jenny and Dolly and Susan resumed their usual occupations-what might be called their household duties. Little Bob played on the sand in sublime indifference, waiting for his mother to prepare some soaked biscuit for him. Susan was overcome by grief and anxiety as she thought of the distress and want which her child might not have the strength to endure.

After putting everything in order inside the cave, Jenny and Dolly came out and joined Mrs. Wolston. Then very sadly they talked of their present situation, which had been so sorely aggravated since the day before. Dolly and Susan were more overcome than the courageous Jenny.

"What will become of us?" Susan asked.

"Don't let us lose heart," Jenny answered, "and above all don't let us discourage our men."

"But we can never get away now," Dolly said. "And when the rainy season comes--"

"I tell you, Dolly, as I told Susan," Jenny answered, "that no good is done by giving up courage."

"How can I keep any hope at all?" Mrs. Wolston exclaimed.

"You must! It's your duty to!" Jenny said.

"Think of your husband; you will increase his misery a thousandfold if you let him see you cry."

"You are strong, Jenny," Dolly said; "you have fought misfortune before. But we--"

"You?" Jenny replied. "Do you forget that Captain Gould and Fritz and Frank and James and John Block will do everything that is possible to save us all?"

"What can they do?" Susan demanded.

"I don't know, Susan, but they will succeed provided we don't hamper them by giving way ourselves to despair!"

"My child! My child!" murmured the poor woman, choked by sobs.

Seeing his mother crying, Bob stood in wonder, with his eyes wide open.

Jenny drew him to her and took him on her knees.

"Mummy was anxious, darling! She called you, and you didn't answer, and then you were playing on the sand, weren't you?"

"Yes," said Bob; "with the boat that Block made for me. But I wanted him to make a little white sail for it, so that it could sail. There are holes full of water in the sand where I can put it. Aunty Dolly promised to make me a sail."

"Yes, Bob dear; you shall have it today," Dolly promised.

"Two sails," the child answered; "two sails like the boat that brought us here."

"Of course," Jenny answered. "Aunty Dolly will make you a lovely sail, and I will make you one, too."

"Thank you, thank you, Jenny," Bob answered, clapping his hands. "But where is our big boat? I can't see it anywhere!"

"It has gone away-fishing," Jenny answered. "It will come back soon, with lots of beautiful fish! Besides, you have got your own; the one that good John Block made for you."

"Yes; but I am going to tell him to make me another, one in which I can sail-with papa and mama, and aunty Dolly and Jenny, and everybody!"

Poor little fellow! He voiced so exactly what was wanted-the replacement of the boat! And how was that to be done?

"Run away again and play, darling," Jenny said to him; "and don't go far away."

"No; over there; quite close, Jenny!"

And he kissed his mother and went bounding away as children of his age will.

"Susan dear, and you, too, Dolly dear," said Jenny, "God will see that that little child is saved! And Bob's rescue means our own! I do beg of you, no more weakness, no more crying! Have faith in Providence as I have, as I have always had!"

So Jenny spoke out of her brave heart. Come what might, she would never despair. If the rainy season set in before the shipwrecked people could leave this coast-and how could they leave it unless some ship took them off? Arrangements would be made to spend a winter there. The cave would give secure protection from the heavy weather. The heaps of sea-weed would give fuel to protect them from the cold. Fishing, hunting perhaps, would suffice to provide them with their daily bread.

It was of the first importance to know whether John Block's fears about the turtles were well founded. Happily they were not. After being away for an hour, the boatswain and Frank came back with their accustomed load of turtles, which had taken refuge under the heap of kelp. But they had not a single egg.

"Never mind, they will lay, good old things," said John Block cheerily.

It was impossible not to smile at the boatswain's little joke. In the course of their walk to the bastion, Captain Gould, Fritz, and James had seen again the impossibility of getting round it in any other way than by sea. Currents ran there, with tremendous force and in both directions. Even in calm weather the violent surf would have prevented any boat from getting close in, and the strongest swimmer might have been carried out to sea or dashed upon the rocks.

So the necessity of getting to the top of the cliff by some other means became more imperative than ever.

"How are we to do it?" said Fritz one day, gazing irritably at the inaccessible crest.

"You can't get out of a prison when its walls are a thousand feet high," was James' answer.

"Unless you tunnel through them," Fritz replied.

"Tunnel through that mass of granite which is probably thicker than it is high?" said James.

"Anyhow, we can't remain in this prison!" exclaimed Fritz, in a burst of impotent but uncontrollable anger.

"Be patient, and have confidence," said Frank again.

"Patience I can have," Fritz retorted, "but confidence-that is another thing."

And indeed on what might confidence be placed? Rescue could only come from a ship passing beyond the bay. And if one came, would it see their signals, the lighting of a huge fire on the beach or on the end of the promontory?

A fortnight had passed since the boat came to land. Several more weeks passed without bringing any change in the situation. As to the food supplies, they were reduced to turtles and their eggs, and to crustaceans, crabs and lobsters, some of which John Block was generally able to catch. It was he who usually occupied himself with the fishing, assisted by Frank. Lines with bent nails for hooks taken from the boat's planks, had rendered possible the capture of various kinds of fish: dorado twelve to fifteen inches long, of a beautiful reddish color and excellent eating, and bass, or salt-water perch. Once even, a large sturgeon was caught with a slip-knot which landed it on the sand.

The dog-fish, plentiful in these waters, were poor eating. But there was obtained from them a grease used to make coarse candies, for which wicks were fashioned out of dry seaweed. Disturbing as the prospect of wintering here might be, thought had to be given to it, and precautions taken against the long and dark days of the rainy season.

The salmon, which used to go up Jackal River in New Switzerland in such numbers at certain times of the year, were not forthcoming here. But one day a school of herrings stranded at the mouth of the little stream. Several hundreds of them were taken, and, smoked over a fire of dry sea-weed, made an important reserve of food.

"Isn't there a saying that herrings bring their own butter?" John Block inquired.

"Well, if so, here are some already cooked, and what I want to know is what we shall do with all these good things!"

Several times during these six weeks attempts had been made to climb to the top of the cliff. As all these attempts were fruitless, Fritz determined to go round the bluff to the east. But he was careful to say nothing of his intention to anyone except John Block. So, on the morning of the 7th of December, the two men went to the creek, under the pretence of collecting turtles at its eastern point.

There, at the foot of the enormous mass of rock, the sea was breaking savagely, and to get round it Fritz must risk his life.

The boatswain vainly did his best to induce him to desist from the idea, and, failing, had no choice but to help him.

After undressing, Fritz fastened a long line around his loins-one of the boat's yard-ropes-gave the other end to John Block, and jumped into the sea.

The risk was twofold-of being caught by the surf and thrown against the base of the bluff, and of being carried away by the current if the line should break.

Twice did Fritz try without success to get free of the waves. It was only at the third attempt that he succeeded in reaching and maintaining a position in which he could look beyond the bluff, and then John Block was obliged to pull him in again to the point-not without a good deal of trouble.

"Well," the boatswain inquired, "what is there beyond?"

The Castaways of the Flag

"Nothing but rocks and more rocks!" Fritz answered as soon as he had recovered his wind. "I only saw a succession of creeks and capes. The cliff goes right on to the north ward."

"I'm not surprised," John Block replied.

When the result of this attempt was made known-one can imagine Jenny's emotions when she heard of it-it seemed as if the last hope had vanished. This island, from which Captain Gould and his boat's company could not escape, was apparently nothing better than an uninhabited and uninhabitable rock!

And this unhappy situation was complicated by so many bitter regrets! But for the mutiny, the passengers on the *Flag* would have reached the fertile domain of the Promised Land a couple of months ago. Think of the anguish of all those who were expecting them and watched in vain for their coming!

Truly these relations and friends of theirs were more to be pitied than Captain Gould and his company. At any rate, the forlorn company knew that their dear ones were safe in New Switzerland.

Thus the future loomed heavy with anxiety, and the present was hard.

A new reason for alarm would have been added if all had known what only Captain Gould and the boatswain knew-that the number of turtles was decreasing perceptibly, in consequence of their daily consumption!

"But perhaps," John Block suggested, "it is because the creatures know of some passage underground through which they can get to the creeks to the east and west; it is a pity we can't follow them."

"Anyhow, Block," Captain Gould replied, "don't say a word to our friends."

"Keep your mind easy, captain. I told you because one can tell you everything."

"And ought to tell me everything, Block!"

Thereafter the boatswain was obliged to fish more assiduously, for the sea would never withhold what the land would soon deny. Of course, if they lived exclusively on fish and molluscs and crustaceans, the general health would suffer. And if illness broke out, that would be the last straw.

The last week of December came. The weather was still fine, except for a few thunderstorms, not so violent as the first one. The heat, sometimes excessive, would have been almost intolerable but for the great shadow thrown over the shore by the cliff, which sheltered it from the sun as it traced its daily arc above the northern horizon.

At this season numbers of birds thronged these waters-not only sea-gulls and divers, sea-mew and frigate birds, which were the usual dwellers on the shore. From time to time flocks of cranes and herons passed, reminding Fritz of his excellent sport round Swan Lake and about the farms in the Promised Land. On the top of the bluff, too, cormorants appeared, like Jenny's bird, now in the poultry-run at Rock Castle, and albatrosses like the one she had sent with her message from the Burning Rock.

These birds kept out of range. When they settled on the promontory it was useless to attempt to get near them, and they flew at full speed above the inaccessible crest of the cliff. One day all the others were called to the beach by a shout from the boatswain.

"Look there! Look there!" he continued to cry, pointing to the edge of the upper plateau.

"What is it?" Fritz demanded.

"Can't you see that row of black specks?" John Block returned.

"They are penguins," Frank replied.

"Yes, they are penguins," Captain Gould declared; "they look no bigger than crows, but that is because they are perched so high up."

"Well," said Fritz, "if those birds have been able to get up on to the plateau, it means that on the other side of the cliff the ascent is practicable."

That seemed certain, for penguins are clumsy, heavy birds, with rudimentary stumps instead of wings. They could not have flown up to the crest. So if the ascent could not be made on the south, it could be on the north. But from lack of a boat in which to go along the shore this hope of reaching the top of the cliff had to be abandoned.

The Castaways of the Flag

Sad, terribly sad, was the Christmas of this most gloomy year! Full of bitterness was the thought of what Christmas might have been in the large hall of Rock Castle, in the midst of the two families, with Captain Gould and John Block.

Yet, in spite of all these trials, the health of the little company was not as yet affected. On the boatswain hardship had no more effect than disappointment.

"I am getting fat," he often said; "yes, I am getting fat! That's what comes of spending one's time doing nothing!"

Doing nothing, alas! Unhappily, in the present situation, there was practically nothing to do!

In the afternoon of the 29th something happened which recalled memories of happier days.

A bird settled on a part of the promontory which was not inaccessible.

It was an albatross, which had probably come a long way, and seemed to be very tired. It lay out on a rock, its legs stretched, its wings folded.

Fritz determined to try to capture this bird. He was clever with the lasso, and he thought he might succeed if he made a running noose with one of the boat's halyards.

A long line was prepared by the boatswain, and Fritz climbed up the promontory as softly as possible.

Everybody watched him.

The bird did not move and Fritz, getting within a few fathoms of it, cast his lasso round its body.

The bird made hardly any attempt to get free when Fritz, who had picked it up in his arms, brought it down to the beach.

Jenny could not restrain a cry of astonishment.

"It is! It is!" she exclaimed, caressing the bird. "I am sure I recognize him!"

"What?" Fritz exclaimed; "you mean-"

"Yes, Fritz, yes! It really is my albatross; my companion on Burning Rock; the one to which I tied the note that fell into your hands."

Could it be? Was not Jenny mistaken? After three whole years, could that same albatross, which had never returned to the island, have flown to this coast?

But Jenny was not mistaken, and all were made quite sure about it when she showed them a little bit of thread still fastened round one of the bird's claws. Of the scrap of cloth on which Fritz had traced his few words of reply, nothing now remained.

If the albatross had come from so far, it was no doubt because these powerful birds can fly vast distances. Quite likely this one had come from the east of the Indian Ocean to these regions of the Pacific possibly more than a thousand miles away!

Much petting was lavished upon the messenger from Burning Rock. It was like a link between the shipwrecked people and their friends in New Switzerland.

Two days later the year 1817 reached its end.

What did the new year hold in store?

Chapter VIII – Little Bob Lost

If Captain Gould was not mistaken in his calculations about the geographical position of the island, the summer season could not have more than another three months to run. After that, winter would arrive, formidable by reason of its cold squalls and furious storms. The faint chance of attracting the attention of some ship out at sea by means of signals would have disappeared. In winter sailors avoid these dangerous waters. But just possibly something would happen before then to modify the situation.

Existence was much what it had been ever since that gloomy 26th of October when the boat was destroyed. The monotony was terribly trying to such active men. With nothing to do but wander about at the foot of the cliff which imprisoned them, tiring their eyes with watching the ever deserted sea, they needed extraordinary moral courage not to give way to despair.

The long, long days were spent in conversation in which Jenny bore the principal part.

The brave young woman loved them all, taxed her ingenuity to keep their minds occupied, and discussed all manner of schemes, as to the utility of which she herself was under no misapprehension.

Sometimes they wondered if the island really lay, as they had supposed, in the west of the Pacific. The boatswain expressed some doubt on this point.

"Is it the albatross's coming that has changed your mind?" the captain asked him one day.

"Well, yes, it has," John Block replied; "and I am right, I think."

"You infer from it that this island lies farther north than we supposed, Block?"

"Yes, captain; and, for all anybody knows, somewhere near the Indian Ocean. An albatross might fly hundreds of miles without resting, but hardly thousands."

' I know that," Captain Gould replied, "but I know, too, that it was to Borupt's interest to take the *Flag* towards the Pacific! As for the week

77

we were shut up in the hold, I thought, and so did you, that the wind was from the west."

"I agree," the boatswain answered, "and yet, this albatross. Has it come from near, or from far?"

"And even supposing you are right, Block, even supposing we were mistaken about the position of this island, and that it really is only a few miles from New Switzerland, isn't that just as bad as if it were hundreds of miles off, seeing that we can't get away from it?"

Captain Gould's conclusion was unfortunately only too reasonable. Everything pointed to the probability of the *Flag* having steered for the Pacific, far, very far, from New Switzerland's waters. And yet what John Block was thinking, others were thinking too. It seemed as if the bird from Burning Rock had brought hope with it.

When the bird recovered from its exhaustion, which it speedily did, it was neither timid nor wild. It was soon walking about the beach, feeding on the berries of the kelp or on fish, which it was very clever in catching, and it showed no desire to fly away.

Sometimes it would fly along the promontory and settle on the top of the cliff, uttering little cries.

"Ah, ha!" the boatswain used to say then. "He is asking us up! If only he could give me the loan of his wings I would willingly undertake to fly up there, and look over the other side. Very likely that side of the coast isn't any better than this one, but at any rate we would know."

Know? Did they not know already, since Fritz had seen nothing but the same arid rocks and the same inaccessible heights beyond the bluff?

One of the albatross's chief friends was little Bob. A comradeship had promptly been established between the child and the bird. They played together on the sand. There was no danger to be apprehended from the teasing of the one or the pecking of the other. When the weather was bad both went into the cave where the albatross had his own corner.

Serious thought had to be given to the chances of a winter here. But for some stroke of good fortune they would have to endure four or five months of bad weather. In these latitudes, in the heart of the Pacific, storms burst with extraordinary violence, and lower the temperature to a serious extent.

The Castaways of the Flag

Captain Gould, Fritz, and John Block talked sometimes of this. It was better to look the perils of the future squarely in the face. Having made up their minds to struggle on, they no longer felt the discouragement which had been caused earlier by the destruction of the boat.

"If only the situation were not aggravated by the presence of the women and the child," Captain Gould said more than once, "if we were only men here."

"All the more reason to do more than we should have done," Fritz rejoined.

One serious question cropped up in these anticipations of the winter: if the cold became severe, and a fire had to be kept up day and night, might not the supply of fuel give out?

Kelp was deposited on the beach by every incoming tide and quickly dried by the sun. But an acrid smoke was produced by the combustion of these sea-weeds, and they could not make use of them to warm the cave. The atmosphere would have been rendered unbearable. So it was thought best to close the entrance with the sails of the boat, fixing them firmly enough to withstand the squalls which beset the cliff during the winter.

There remained the problem of lighting the inside of the cave when the weather should preclude the possibility of working outside.

The boatswain and Frank, assisted by Jenny and Dolly, made many rude candies out of the grease from the dog-fish which swarmed in the creek and were very easy to catch.

John Block melted this grease and so obtained a kind of oil which coagulated as it cooled. Since he had at his disposal none of the cotton grown by M. Zermatt, he was obliged to content himself with the fibre of the laminariae, which furnished practicable wicks.

There was also the question of clothes, and that was a different question indeed.

"It's pretty clear," said the boatswain one day, "that when you are shipwrecked and cast on a desert island it is prudent to have a ship at your disposal in which you can find every thing you want. One makes a poor job of it otherwise!"

They all agreed. That was how the *Landlord* had been the salvation of the people in New Switzerland.

In the afternoon of the 17th an incident of which no one could have foreseen the consequence caused the most intense anxiety.

As already mentioned, Bob found great pleasure in playing with the albatross. When he was amusing himself on the shore his mother kept a constant watch upon him, to see that he did not go far away, for he was fond of scrambling about among the low rocks of the promontory and running away from the waves. But when he stayed with the bird in the cave there was no risk in leaving him by himself.

It was about three o'clock. James Wolston was helping the boatswain to arrange the spars to support the heavy curtain in front of the entrance to the cave. Jenny and Susan and Dolly were sitting in the corner by the stove on which the little kettle was boiling, and were busy mending their clothes.

It was nearly time for Bob's luncheon.

Mrs. Wolston called the child.

Bob did not answer.

Susan went down to the beach and called louder, but still got no reply.

Then the boatswain called out:

"Bob! Bob! It's dinner time!"

The child did not appear, and he could not be seen running about the shore.

"He was here only a minute ago," James declared.

"Where the deuce can he be?" John Block said to himself, as he went towards the promontory.

Captain Gould, Fritz, and Frank were walking along the foot of the cliff.

Bob was not with them.

The boatswain made a trumpet of his hands and called out several times:

"Bob! Bob!"

The child remained invisible.

James came up to the captain and the two brothers.

"You haven't seen Bob, have you?" he asked in a very anxious voice.

"No," Frank answered.

"I saw him half an hour ago," Fritz declared; "he was playing with the albatross."

And all began to call him, turning in every direction.

It was in vain.

Then Fritz and James went to the promontory, climbed the nearest rocks, and looked all over the creek.

Neither child nor bird was there.

Both went back to the others. Mrs. Wolston was pale with fear.

"Have you looked inside the cave?" Captain Gould asked.

Fritz made one spring to the cave and searched every corner of it, but came back without the child.

Mrs. Wolston was distracted. She went to and fro like a mad woman. The little boy might have slipped among the rocks, or fallen into the sea. The most alarming suppositions were permissible since Bob Had not been found.

So the search had to be prosecuted without a moment's delay along the beach and as far as the creek.

"Fritz and James," said Captain Gould, "come with me along the foot of the cliff. Do you think Bob could have got buried in a heap of sea-weed?"

"Yes, you go," said the boatswain, "while Mr. Frank and I go and search the creek."

"And the promontory," Frank added. "It is possible that Bob may have taken it into his head to go climbing there and have fallen into

some hole."

So they separated, some going to the right, some to the left. Jenny and Dolly stayed with Mrs. Wolston and tried to allay her anxiety.

Half an hour later, all were back again, after a fruitless search. Nowhere in the bay was any trace of the child, and all their calling had been without result.

Susan's grief broke out. She sobbed in anguish and had to be carried, against her will, into the cave. Her husband, who went with her, could not utter a word.

Outside, Frank said:

"The child can't possibly be lost! I tell you again, I saw him on the shore scarcely an hour ago, and he was not near the sea. He had a string in his hand, with a pebble at the end of it, and was playing with the albatross."

"By the way, where is the bird?" Frank asked, looking round.

"Yes; where is he?" John Block echoed.

"Can they have disappeared together?" Captain Gould inquired.

"It looks like it," Fritz replied.

They looked in every direction, and especially towards the rocks where the bird was accustomed to perch.

It was not to be seen, nor could its cry be heard-a cry easily distinguishable from the noises of the divers, gulls, and sea-mews.

The albatross might have flown above the cliff and made for some other eminence along the coast. But the little boy could not have flown away. Yet he might have been capable of climbing along the promontory after the bird. This explanation was hardly admissible, however, after the search that Frank and the boatswain had made.

Yet it was impossible not to see some connection between Bob's disappearance and that of the albatross. They hardly ever separated, and now they were both lost together!

Evening drew on. The father and mother were in terrible grief. Susan was so agitated that they feared for her reason. Jenny, Dolly, Captain Gould and the others, did not know what next to do. When they reflected that if the child had fallen into some hole he would have to stay there all night, they began to search again. A fire of sea-weed was lighted at the far end of the promontory, to be a guide for the child in case he should have gone to the back of the creek. But after remaining afoot until the last possible minute of the evening, they had to give up hope of finding Bob. And what were the chances of their being more successful next day!

Ali went back into the cave, but not to sleep. How could they sleep? First one, and then another went out, watched, listened through the rippling of the tide, and then came back and sat down again without saying a word.

It was the most sorrowful, heart-breaking night of all that Captain Gould and his company had passed upon this deserted coast.

About two o'clock in the morning, the sky, which had been brilliant with stars until then, began to be overcast. The breeze was now in the north, and the clouds from that quarter gathered overhead. Not yet very thick, they chased each other with ever increasing speed, and east and west of the cliff the sea must certainly be rough.

It was the time when the flood brought up on to the beach the rollers of the rising tide.

Just at this moment Mrs. Wolston got up, and before she could be stopped she rushed out of the cave in delirium, shrieking:

"My child! My child!"

Force had to be used to get her back again. James, who had caught his wife up, took her in his arms and carried her back, more dead than alive.

The unhappy mother remained stretched out on the heap of kelp where Bob usually slept by her side. Jenny and Dolly tried to bring her round, but it was only after great efforts on their part that she recovered consciousness.

Throughout the remainder of the night the wind moaned incessantly round the top of the cliff. A score of times the men searched all over the shore, fearing always that the incoming tide might lay a little corpse upon the sand.

But there was nothing, nothing! Could the child have been carried out to sea by the waves?

About four o'clock when the ebb tide was just setting in after the slack, light appeared in the east.

At this moment Fritz, who was leaning against the back of the cave, thought he heard a kind of cry behind the wall. He listened, and fearing that he might be mistaken, went up to the captain.

"Come with me!" he said.

Without knowing, without even asking what Fritz wanted, Captain Gould went with him.

"Listen!" said Fritz.

Captain Gould listened intently.

"I can hear a bird's cry," he said.

"Yes, a bird's cry!" Fritz declared.

"Then there is a hollow behind the wall."

"There must be; and perhaps a passage communicating with the outside; how else is it to be explained?"

"You are right, Fritz!'

John Block was told. He put his ear against the wall, and said positively:

"It's the albatross's cry: I recognize it."

"And if the albatross is there," said Fritz, "little Bob must be there too."

"But how could they both have got in?" the captain asked.

"That we will find out," John Block replied. Frank and Jenny and Dolly were now told. James and his wife recovered a little hope.

"He is there! He is there!" Susan said over and over again.

John Block had lighted one of the thick candies. That the albatross was behind the wall nobody could doubt, for its cry continued to be heard.

The Castaways of the Flag

But just before looking to see if it had slipped in by some opening outside, it was necessary to make sure that the back wall had no orifice.

Candle in hand, the boatswain began to examine this wall.

John Block could only see on its surface a few fissures which were too narrow for the albatross or Bob to get through. But at the bottom a hole, twenty to twenty-five inches wide, was hollowed out in the ground, a hole big enough to take the bird and the child.

Meantime, however, the albatross's cry had ceased, and all were afraid that Captain Gould, the boatswain, and Fritz must have been mistaken.

Then Jenny took John Block's place, and stooping down level with the hole, she called the bird several times. The albatross knew her voice as well as it knew her caress.

A cry answered her, and almost immediately the bird came out through the hole.

"Bob! Bob!" Jenny called again.

The child did not answer, did not appear. Was he not with the bird behind the wall? His mother could not restrain a cry of despair.

"Wait!" said the boatswain.

He crouched down and enlarged the hole, throwing the sand out behind him. In a few minutes he had made the hole large enough for him to squeeze into it.

A minute later he brought out little Bob, who had fainted, but who was not long in recovering consciousness under his mother's kisses.

Chapter IX – Bob Found

It took Mrs. Wolston some time to recover from her terrible shock. But Bob was restored to her, and that comforted her.

It appeared that Bob, playing with the albatross, had followed it to the back of the cave. The bird made its way in through the narrow passage, and Bob went after it. A dark excavation opened out at the end, and when the little fellow wanted to get out of this he found that he could not. At first he called, but his calls were not heard. Then he lost consciousness, and nobody knows what might have happened if by the luckiest chance Fritz had not happened to hear the cry of the albatross.

"Well," said the boastwain," now that Bob is in his mother's arms again, everything is for the best. Thanks to him we have discovered another cave. It is true we haven't any use to put it to. The first one was enough for us, and as a matter of fact we ask nothing better than to get away from that one."

"But I want to find out how far it runs back," Captain Gould remarked.

"Right to the other side of the cliff, do you fancy, captain?"

"Who can tell, Block?"

"All right," the boatswain answered. "But even supposing it does run through the cliff, what shall we find on the other side? Sand, rocks, creeks, promontories, and as much green stuff as I can cover with my hat."

"That's very likely," Fritz replied. "But none the less we must look."

"We'll look, Mr. Fritz; we'll look. Looking costs nothing, as the saying is."

The investigation might have such priceless results that it had to be undertaken without delay.

The captain, Fritz, and Frank went back to the end of the cave. The boatswain walked behind them, armed with several big candles. To make the way easier, those in front enlarged the aperture by removing some more of the stones which had fallen into it.

The Castaways of the Flag

A quarter of an hour sufficed to make the opening large enough. None of them had put on flesh since they had landed. Only the boatswain had not lost weight since he had left the *Flag.*

When they had all got through, the candles gave sufficient light for them to examine this second excavation.

It was deeper than the first one, but much narrower, a hundred feet or so long, ten or twelve feet in diameter, and about the same height. It was possible that other passages branched off from it and formed a kind of labyrinth inside the massive cliff. Captain Gould wondered whether one of these branches might not perhaps lead, if not to the top of the cliff, at any rate beyond the bluff or the bastion.

When Captain Gould urged this point again John Block replied:

"It certainly is possible. Who knows whether we shan't reach the top through the inside, although we couldn't do so outside?"

When they had gone some fifty feet through this passage, which gradually got narrower, Captain Gould, the boatswain, and Fritz came to a wall of rock before which they were obliged to stop.

John Block passed the light all over its surface from the ground to the vault, but found only narrow fissures into which the hand could not be put. So there was no more hope of penetrating further through the solid mass.

Nor did the side walls of the passage disclose any aperture. This second excavation beyond the first cave was the sole discovery resulting from the incident.

"Well," said Captain Gould, "it's not by this way that we shall get through the cliff."

"Nor over it," added the boatswain.

And, having made sure of that, they could do nothing but go back.

As a matter of fact, although it was rather disappointing not to find any inner passage, nobody had thought it likely.

And yet when Captain Gould and John Block and Fritz got back, they had a feeling of being more confined than ever on this shore.

During the next few days the weather, very fine hitherto, showed signs of changing. Light clouds, which soon grew thicker, obscured the blue sky, blown over the plateau above by a northerly breeze which, in the evening of the 22nd of January, strengthened until it blew a gale.

Coming from that quarter, the wind was no menace to Turtle Bay. Sheltered by the cliff, the bay was not exposed to the breakers, as it had been in the violent storm which had caused the destruction of the boat. The sea would remain calm along the shore, not getting the force of the wind nearer than a good mile and a half from the coast. Even if a hurricane burst there would be nothing to fear.

A heavy thunderstorm broke on the night of the 22nd. About one o'clock in the morning everybody was awakened suddenly by a crash of thunder that made a more appalling noise than a cannon fired at the mouth of the cave could have done.

Fritz Frank, and the boatswain sprang from their corners, and rushed to the door.

"The lightning struck quite close by." said Frank.

"At the crest of the cliff above us, most likely," replied John Block, going a few steps outside.

Susan and Dolly, who were always greatly affected by thunderstorms, as many people of nervous temperament are, had followed Jenny outside the cave.

"Well?" Dolly inquired.

"There is no danger, Dolly, dear," Frank answered. "Go back and close your eyes and ears."

But Jenny was just saying to her husband, who had come up to her:

"What a smell of smoke, Fritz!"

"That's not surprising," said the boatswain.

"There is the fire-over there."

"Where?" Captain Gould asked sharply.

"On that heap of sea-weed at the foot of the cliff."

The Castaways of the Flag

The lightning had set fire to the heap of dry weed. In a few minutes the flames had spread to the mass of sea-weeds collected at the base of the cliff. It burned up like straw, crackling in the breeze, eddying about like will-of-the wisps, and spreading an acrid smoke over the whole beach.

Fortunately, the entrance to the cave was clear, and the fire could not reach it.

"That's our reserve burning!" John Block exclaimed.

"Can't we save any of it?" said Fritz.

"I fear not!" Captain Gould replied.

The flames spread so rapidly that it was impossible to remove to safety the heaps which furnished the only fuel the shipwrecked people had.

True, the quantity deposited by the sea was inexhaustible. The stuff would continue to be thrown up, but it would take a long time for such a quantity to accumulate. The incoming tide deposited a few armfuls twice in every twenty-four hours. What had lain on the beach was the harvest of many years. And who could say that, in the few weeks remaining before the rainy season, the tide would have thrown up enough for the winter's need?

In less than a quarter of an hour the line of fire had ringed the whole circle of the shore, and except for a few heaps along the promontory there was nothing left.

This fresh hammer-blow of evil fortune aggravated the situation, already so disturbing.

"Upon my word, it's no go!"

And coming from the lips of the boatswain, who was always so confident, the words had exceptional significance.

But they would not make the walls of the prison fall down, to allow the prisoners to escape!

Next morning the weather, though no longer thundery, was still unsettled, and the north wind continued to sweep the plateau fiercely.

Their first business was to see whether the sea-weeds piled up along the bastion had been spared by the fire. They had been partially.

The men brought back in their arms enough to last for a week, exclusive of what the tides would bring up every day.

While the wind continued to blow from the north these floating masses would, of course, be carried to sea.

But as soon as it veered round to the south again, the harvest could be gathered more abundantly.

Nevertheless, Captain Gould pointed out that some precautions would have to be taken for the future.

"Quite right, captain," John Block answered; "it would be a good plan to put what is left of the sea-weed under cover, in case we have to winter here."

"Why not store it in the second cave that we have just discovered?" Fritz suggested.

That seemed to be expressly indicated, and that day, before noon, Fritz resolved to go back into the cave, in order to examine its nature and arrangements inside. Provided with a candle, he crept through the narrow opening communicating between the two caves. Who could say if the second one had not some means of egress beyond the mass of rock?

But just as he reached the far end of the long passage, Fritz felt a fresher breath of air, and at the same moment his ear detected a continual whistling sound.

"Wind!" he muttered. "That's wind!"

He put his face near the wall, and his hand found several fissures in it.

"Wind!" he said again. "It certainly is wind! It gets in here when it blows from the north. So there is a passage, either on the side or at the top of the cliff! But then, on this side, it would mean that there is a communication with the northern flank of the cliff!"

Just at that moment the candle which Fritz was passing along the wall went out suddenly, in a stronger draught blowing through out of the fissures.

Fritz did not wait for anything more. He was convinced. If one got through this wall one would have free access to the outside!

To crawl back to the cave where all were waiting for him, to tell them of his discovery, to take them back again with him, and make sure that he was right, was only the work of minutes.

In a few minutes more Fritz, followed by Captain Gould, John Block, and James, went from the first cave into the second. They lighted their way by candles which, on this occasion, they were careful not to put too near the wall at the far end.

Fritz was not mistaken. Fresh air was blowing freely through the passage.

Then the boatswain, passing the light along the level of the ground, noticed that the passage was closed only by a heap of stones which had no doubt fallen right down a kind of natural shaft.

"The door!" be exclaimed. "There's the door! And no need of a key to open it with! Ah, captain, you were in the right of it after all!"

"Get on to it! Get on to it!" was all Captain Gould's reply.

It was easy to clear the passage of the obstructing stones. They passed them from hand to hand, quite a lot of them, for the heap was five or six feet above the ground level. As the work proceeded the current of air became stronger. There most certainly was a sort of gorge carved out inside the mass of the rock.

A quarter of an hour was enough to clear the passage entirely.

Fritz was the first through, and, followed by the others, he went ten or twelve steps up a very steep slope, dimly lighted.

There was no vertical shaft. A gorge, five or six feet wide and open to the sky, wound between two walls which rose to an immense height, and a strip of blue sky formed its ceiling. It was down this gorge the wind rushed, to creep through the fissures in the wall at the end of the passage.

And so the cliff was rent right through! But where did the rift open out?

They could not tell until they had reached the far end of it, supposing they found it possible to do so.

But for all that they stood like prisoners before whom the gaol doors have just opened!

It was barely eight o'clock, and there was plenty of time. They did not even discuss the question of sending Fritz or the boatswain on in advance to explore. Everyone wanted to go up the passage at once, without losing a minute.

"But we must take some provisions," Jenny said. "Who can tell whether we shall not be away longer than we think?"

"Besides," Fritz added, "have we any idea where we are going?"

"Outside," the boatswain replied.

The simple word, so exactly expressing the general sentiment, answered everything.

But Captain Gould insisted that they should have breakfast first, also that they should take provisions for several days with them, in case they should be delayed.

Breakfast was hurried through. After four months passed in this bay, they were naturally in a hurry to find out whether their situation had improved, perhaps even changed entirely.

Besides, there would still be time to come back, if the upper plateau proved to be as barren as the shore, if it were unsuitable for a settlement, if from the extreme summit no other land were to be seen in the proximity. If the castaways from the *Flag* found they had landed on an island or islet, they would return to the cave and make their arrangements to meet the winter there.

Directly the meal was finished the men took the bundles of provisions. The first cave was left, and, with the albatross walking beside Jenny, all went through the mouth of the passage.

When they came to the mouth of the gorge, Fritz and Frank went through first. After them came Jenny, Dolly, and Susan, holding little Bob's hand.

Captain Gould and James came next, and John Block closed the rear.

The Castaways of the Flag

At first the gorge was so narrow that they had to walk in single file.

It was really nothing but a cleft in the solid rock, running in a northerly direction between two vertical walls which rose to a height of eight or nine hundred feet.

After a hundred yards or so in a straight line, the ground began to slope upwards rather steeply. The way must be a long one, for if it did debouch upon the plateau it would have had to make up the five hundred feet or so from the level of the beach to the upper part of the cliff. Moreover, the journey was soon lengthened by the twists and turns of the path. It was like the abrupt and capricious twisting of a labyrinth inside the mass of rock. But judging from the light that spread from above, Harry Gould believed that the general direction of the gorge was from south to north. The lateral walls gradually drew further apart, rendering the march much easier.

About ten o'clock they were obliged to call a halt to allow everyone to recover breath. They stopped in a sort of semi-circular cavity, above which a much larger slice of the sky was visible.

Captain Gould estimated that this spot was about two hundred feet above the level of the sea.

"At this rate," he remarked, "it will take us five or six hours to reach the top."

"Well," Fritz replied, "it will still be broad daylight when we get there, and if need be we shall have time to get down again before night."

"Quite true, Fritz," the captain replied, "but how can we be sure that the gorge is not lengthened by an even greater number of turnings?"

"Or that it does not come out upon the cliff?" Frank added.

"Whether it's at the top or the side of the cliff, let us take things as they come," the boatswain put in. "Above, if it is above, below, if it is below! After all, this don't matter much!"

After a rest of half an hour, the march was resumed. The gorge, which wound about ever more and more, and now measured ten to twelve feet across, was carpeted with a sandy soil, scattered with pebbles, and without a sign of vegetation. It seemed as though the summit must be an arid waste, for otherwise some seed or germ would have been carried down by the rain and would have sprouted. But there was nothing here-not even a patch of lichen or moss.

About two o 'clock in the afternoon another halt was called for rest and refreshment. They all sat down in a kind of clearing where the walls widened out like a bell, and over which the sun was passing on its downward way to the west. The height now attained was estimated at seven or eight hundred feet, which justified the hope of reaching the upper plateau.

At three o'clock the journey was resumed. The difficulties became momentarily greater. The slope was very steep, the ground strown with landslips which made climbing hard, and there were large stones which slipped and bounded down. The gorge, which had widened out considerably, now formed a ravine, with sides still rising two or three hundred feet in height. They had to help one another, and pull each other up by the arms. Everything pointed to the possibility of reaching the plateau now. And the albatross spread out its wings and rose with a spring, as if inviting them to follow. Oh! If only they could have followed in its flight!

At last, after incredible efforts, a little before five o'clock, they all stood on the top of the cliff.

To south, to east, to west, nothing at all was to be seen-nothing but the vast expanse of ocean!

Northwards, the plateau extended over an area which could not be estimated, for its boundary crest could not be seen. Did it present a perpendicular wall on that side, fronting the sea? Would they have to go to the far end of it, to see the horizon of the sea in that direction?

Altogether, it was a disappointing sight for people who had hoped to set foot upon some fertile, verdant, wooded region. The same arid desolation reigned here as at Turtle Bay, which was perhaps less depressing, if not less sterile, since mosses did gem it here and there, and there were plenty of sea-weeds on its sandy shore.

And when they turned towards the east and the west, they looked in vain for the outlines of a continent or island. Everything went to show that this was a lonely islet in the middle of these wastes of water.

The Castaways of the Flag

Not a word was uttered by anyone before this dashing of their last hopes. These ghastly solitudes offered no resources. There was nothing to do but descend the ravine, get back to the shore, go into the cave again, settle down there for the long winter months, and wait for rescue from outside!

It was now five o'clock, and there was no time to be lost before the darkness of evening fell. In the gathering shades the walking would not be easy.

Yet, since the northern part of the plateau had still to be explored, it seemed best to make the exploration now. Might it not even be well to camp for the night among the rocks scattered all over the surface? But perhaps that would not be prudent. If the weather changed, where could shelter be found? Prudence required that they should go back without delay.

Then Fritz made a suggestion.

"Jenny, dear, let James and Frank take you back to the cave with Dolly and Mrs. Wolston and the little chap. You can't spend the night on the cliff. Captain Gould, John Block, and I will stay here, and directly it is light tomorrow we will finish our exploration."

Jenny did not answer, and Susan and Dolly seemed to be consulting her with their eyes.

"What Fritz suggests is wise," Frank put in; "and besides, what good can we hope to do by staying here?"

Jenny continued to keep silence, with her eyes fixed upon the vast ocean which spread over three-quarters of the horizon, looking perhaps for the sight of a sail, telling herself that a light might appear in the far offing.

The sun was sinking rapidly already, among clouds driven from the north, and it would mean at least two hours' march through dense darkness to reach Turtle Bay.

Fritz began again:

"Jenny, I beg you, go! No doubt tomorrow will be enough for us. We shall be back in the evening."

95

Jenny cast a last look all round her. All had risen, ready to make a start. The faithful albatross was fluttering from rock to rock, while the other birds, sea-mews, gulls and divers, flew back to their holes in the cliff, uttering parting screams.

The young woman realized that she must do as her husband advised, and regretfully she said:

"Let us go."

Suddenly the boatswain sprang to his feet, and making an ear-trumpet of his hand, listened intently.

A report, muffled by the distance, was audible from the north.

"A gun!" exclaimed John Block.

Chapter X – The Flag On The Peak!

All stood motionless, their hearts tense with excitement, their eyes turned towards the northern horizon, listening intently, scarcely breathing.

In the distance a few more shots rang out, the sound borne to them on the faint breath of the breeze.

"It's a ship passing off the coast!" said Captain Gould at length.

"Yes; those reports can only come from a ship," John Block replied; "when night falls, perhaps we shall see her lights."

"But couldn't those shots have been fired on land?" Jenny suggested.

"On land, Jenny dear?" Fritz exclaimed.

"You mean there may be some land near this island?"

"I think it is more likely that there is some ship off there to the northward," Captain Gould said again.

"Why should it have fired the gun?" James asked.

"Yes, why?" Jenny echoed him.

If the second surmise were the right one, it followed that the ship could not be very far from the shore. Perhaps when it was quite dark they would be able to distinguish the flashes from the guns, if they were fired again. They might also see her lights before long. But, since the sound of the guns had come from the north, it was quite possible that the ship would remain invisible, since the sea in that direction could not be seen.

No longer did any one think of going through the ravine, back to Turtle Bay. Whatever the weather might be, they would all remain where they were until day. Unfortunately, in the event of a ship coming down on the west or east, lack of wood would prevent them from lighting a fire to signal it.

Those distant reports had stirred their hearts to the very depths. They seemed united by them once more to their kind, felt as though this island were now not so utterly isolated.

97

Jules Verne

They would have liked to go at once to the far end of the plateau, and to watch the sea to the northward, whence the cannon shots had come. But the evening was getting on, and night would fall quite soon-a night without moon or stars, darkened by the low clouds that the breeze was chasing to the south. They could not venture among the rocks in darkness. It would be difficult enough by day; it was impossible by night.

So it became necessary to settle themselves for the night where they were, and everyone got busy. After a long search the boatswain discovered a kind of recess, a space between two rocks, where Jenny, Susan, Dolly, and the little boy could lie close to the ground, as there was no sand or sea-weed for them to lie on. They would at least have shelter from the wind if it should freshen, even shelter from the rain if the clouds broke.

The provisions were taken from the bags and all ate. There was food for several days, in any case. And might not all fear of spending a winter in Turtle Bay soon be banished for ever?

Night fell-an endless night it seemed, whose long drawn hours no one could ever forget, except little Bob, who slept in his mother's arms. Utter darkness reigned. From the sea-coast the lights of a ship would have been visible several miles out at sea.

Captain Gould, and most of the others, insisted on remaining afoot until daybreak. Their eyes incessantly wandered over the east and west and south, in the hope of seeing a vessel passing off the island, and not without fears that she might leave it astern, never to return to it. Had they been in Turtle Bay at this moment, they would have lighted a fire upon the end of the promontory. Here, that was impossible.

No light shone out before the return of dawn, no report broke the silence of the night, no ship came in sight of the island.

The men began to wonder whether they had not been mistaken, if they had not taken for the sound of cannon what might only have been the roar of some distant storm.

"No, no," Fritz insisted, "we were not mistaken! It really was a cannon firing out there in the north, a good long way away."

98

The Castaways of the Flag

"I'm sure of it," the boatswain replied. "But why should they be firing guns?" James Wolston urged.

"Either in salute or in self-defence," Fritz answered.

"Perhaps some savages have landed on the island and made an attack," Frank suggested.

"Anyhow," the boatswain answered, "it wasn't savages who fired those guns."

"So the island would be inhabited by Americans or Europeans?" James inquired.

"Well, to begin with, is it only an island?" Captain Gould replied. "How do we know what is beyond this cliff? Are we perhaps upon some very large island?"

"A very large island in this part of the Pacific?" Fritz rejoined. "Which one? I don't see-"

"In my opinion," John Block remarked, with much good sense, "it is useless to argue about all that. The truth is we don 't know whether our island is in the Pacific or the Indian Ocean. Let us have a little patience until dawn, which will break quite soon, and then we will go and see what there is up there to the northward."

"Perhaps everything-perhaps nothing!" said James.

"Well," the boatswain retorted, "it will be something to know which!"

About five o 'clock the first glimmer of dawn began to show. Low on the horizon the east grew pale. The weather was very calm, for the wind had dropped towards morning. The clouds which had been chased by the breeze were now replaced by a veil of mist, through which the sun eventually broke. The whole sky gradually cleared. The streak of light drawn sharply across the east grew wider-spread over the line of sky and sea. The glorious sun appeared, throwing long streamers of light over the surface of the waters.

Eagerly all eyes traveled over so much of the ocean as was visible.

But no vessel was to be seen!

99

Jules Verne

At this moment Captain Gould was joined by Jenny, Dolly, and by Susan Wolston, who was holding her child's hand.

The albatross fluttered to and fro, hopped from rock to rock, and sometimes went quite far off to the northward, as if it were pointing out the way.

"It looks as if he were showing us where to go," said Jenny.

"We must follow him!" Dolly exclaimed.

"Not until we have had breakfast," Captain Gould replied. "We may have several hours' marching in front of us, and we must keep up our strength."

They shared the provisions hurriedly, so impatient were they to be off, and before seven o'clock they were moving towards the north.

It was most difficult walking among the rocks. Captain Gould and the boatswain, in advance, pointed out the practicable paths. Then Fritz came helping Jenny, Frank helping Dolly, and James helping Susan and little Bob.

Nowhere did the foot encounter grass or sand. It was all a chaotic accumulation of stones, what might have been a vast field of scattered rocks or moraines. Over it birds were flying, frigate-birds, sea-mews, and seaswallows, in whose flight the albatross sometimes joined.

They marched for an hour, at the cost of immense fatigue, and had accomplished little more than two miles, steadily up hill. There was no change in the appearance of the nature of the plateau.

It was absolutely necessary to call a halt in order to get a little rest.

Fritz then suggested that he should go on ahead with Captain Gould and John Block. That would spare the others fresh fatigue.

The proposal was unanimously rejected. They would not separate. They all wanted to be there when-or if-the sea became visible in the northward.

The march was resumed about nine o'clock. The mist tempered the beat of the sun. At this season it might have been insupportable on this stony waste, on which the rays fell almost vertically at noon.

The Castaways of the Flag

While still extending towards the north, the plateau was widening out to east and west, and the sea, which so far had been visible in both these directions, would soon be lost to sight. And still there was not a tree, not a trace of vegetation, nothing but the same sterility and solitude. A few low hills rose here and there ahead.

At eleven o'clock a kind of cone showed its naked peak, towering some three hundred feet above this portion of the plateau.

"We must get to the top of that," said Jenny.

"Yes," Fritz replied; "from there we shall be able to see over a much wider horizon. But it may be a rough climb!"

It probably would be, but so irresistible was the general desire to ascertain the actual situation that no one would have consented to remain behind, however great the fatigue might be. Yet who could tell whether these poor people were not marching to a last disappointment, to the shattering of their last hope?

They resumed their journey towards the peak, which now was about half a mile away. Every step was difficult, and progress was painfully slow among the hundreds of rocks which must be scrambled over or gone round. It was more like a chamois track than a footpath. The boatswain insisted on carrying little Bob, and his mother gave the child to him. Fritz and Jenny, Frank and Dolly, and James and Susan kept near together, that the men might help the women over the dangerous bits.

It was past two o 'clock in the afternoon when the base of the cone was reached. They had taken three hours to cover less than a mile and three quarters since the last halt. But they were obliged to rest again.

The stop was of short duration, and in twenty minutes the climbing began.

It had occurred to Captain Gould to go round the peak, to avoid a tiring climb. But its base was seen to be impassable, and, after all, the height was not great.

At the outset the foot found hold upon a soil where scanty plants were growing, clumps of stonecrops to which the fingers could cling.

Half an hour sufficed to bring them half-way up the peak. Then Fritz, who was in front, let a cry of surprise escape him.

All stopped, looking at him.

"What is that, up there?" he said, pointing to the extreme top of the cone.

A stick was standing upright there, a stick five or six feet long, fixed between the highest rocks.

"Can it be a branch of a tree, with all the leaves stripped off?" said Frank.

"No; that is not a branch," Captain Gould declared.

"It is a stick-a walking-stick!" Fritz declared. "A stick which has been set up there."

"And to which a flag has been fastened," the boatswain added; "and the flag is still there!"

A flag at the summit of this peak!

Yes; and the breeze was beginning to stir the flag, although from this distance the colors could not be identified.

"Then there are inhabitants on this island!" Frank exclaimed.

"Not a doubt of it!" Jenny declared.

"Or if not," Fritz went on, "it is clear, at any rate, that someone has taken possession of it."

"What island is this, then?" James Wolston demanded.

"Or, rather, what flag is this?" Captain Gould added.

"An English flag!" the boatswain cried.

"Look: red bunting with the yacht in the corner!"

The wind had just spread out the flag, and it certainly was a British flag.

How they sprang from rock to rock! A hundred and fifty feet still separated them from the summit, but they were no longer conscious of fatigue, did not try to recover their wind, but hurried up without stopping, carried along by what seemed supernatural strength!

At length, just before three o'clock, Captain Gould and his companions stood side by side on the top of the peak.

Their disappointment was bitter when they turned their eyes towards the north.

A thick mist hid the horizon. It was impossible to discover whether the plateau ended on this side in a perpendicular cliff, as it did at Turtle Bay, or whether it spread much further beyond. Through this dense fog nothing could be seen. Above the layer of vapor the sky was still bright with the rays of the sun, now beginning to decline into the west.

Well, they would camp there and wait until the breeze had driven the fog away! Not one of them would go back without having examined the northern portion of the island!

For was there not a British flag there, floating in the breeze? Did it not say as plainly as words that this land was known, that it must figure in latitude and longitude on the English charts?

And those guns they had heard the day before, who could say that they did not come from ships saluting the flag as they moved by? Who could say that there was not some harbor on this coast, that there were not ships at anchor there at this very moment?

And, even if this land were merely a small islet, would there be anything wonderful in Great Britain having taken possession of it, when it lay on the confines of the Indian and the Pacific Oceans? Alternatively, why should it not belong to the Australian continent, so little of which was known in this direction, which was part of the British dominions?

As they talked a bird's cry rang out, followed by a rapid beating of wings.

It was Jenny's albatross, which had just taken flight, and was speeding away through the mists towards the north.

Whither was the bird going? Towards some distant shore?

Its departure produced a feeling of depression, even of anxiety. It seemed like a desertion.

But time was passing. The intermittent breeze was not strong enough to disperse the fog, whose heavy scrolls were rolling at the base of the cone. Would the night fall before the northern horizon had been laid bare to view?

But no; all hope was not yet lost. As the mists began to decrease, Fritz was able to make out that the cone dominated, not a cliff, but long slopes, which probably extended as far as the level of the sea.

Then the wind freshened, the folds of the flag stiffened, and, nearly level with the mists, everyone could see the declivity for a distance of a hundred yards.

It was no longer a mere accumulation of rocks, it was the other side of a mountain, where showed growths on which they had not set eyes for many a long month!

How they feasted their sight on these wide stretches of verdure, on the shrubs, aloes, mastic-trees, and myrtles which were growing everywhere! No; they would not wait for the fog to disperse, and besides, it was imperative that they should reach the base of the mountain before night enveloped them in its shadows!

But now, eight or nine hundred feet below, through the rifts in the mist, appeared the top of the foliage of a forest which extended for several miles; then a vast and fertile plain, strown with clumps of trees and groves, with broad meadows and vast grass-lands traversed by water-courses, the largest of which ran eastwards towards a bay in the coast-line.

On the east and west, the sea extended to the furthest limit of the horizon. Only on the north was it wanting to make of this land, not an islet, but a large island.

Finally, very far away, could be seen the faint outlines of a rocky rampart running from west to east. Was that the edge of a coast?

"Let us go! Let us go!" cried Fritz.

"Yes; let us go!" Frank echoed him. "We shall be down before night."

"And we will pass the night in the shelter of the trees," Captain Gould added.

The last mists cleared away. Then the ocean was revealed over a distance which might be as much as eighteen or twenty miles.

This was an island-it was certainly an island!

They then saw that the northern coast was indented by three hays of unequal size, the largest of which lay to the north-west, another to the north, while the smallest opcned to the north-east, and was more deeply cut into the coast-line than the other two. The arm of the sea which gave access to it was bounded by two distant capes, one of which had at its end a lofty promontory.

No other land showed out to sea. Not a sail appeared on the horizon.

Looking back towards the south the eye was held by the top of the crest of the cliff which enclosed Turtle Bay, five miles or so away.

What a contrast between the desert region which Captain Gould and his companions had just crossed and the land which now lay before their eyes! Here was a fertile and variegated champaign, forests, plains, everywhere the luxuriant vegetation of the tropics! But nowhere was there a hamlet, or a village, or a single habitation.

And then a cry-a cry of sudden revelation which he could not have restrained-broke from the breast of Fritz, while both his arms were stretched out towards the north.

"New Switzerland!"

"Yes; New Switzerland!" Frank cried in his turn.

"New Switzerland!" echoed Jenny and Dolly, in tones broken by emotion.

And so, in front of them, beyond that forest, and beyond those prairies, the rocky barrier that they could see was the rampart through which the defile of Cluse opened on to the Green Valley! Beyond lay the Promised Land, with its woods and farms and Jackal River! There was Falconhurst in the heart of its mangrove wood, and beyond Rock Castle and the trees in its orchards! That bay on the left was Pearl Bay, and farther away, like a small black speck, was the Burning Rock,

105

crowned with the smoke from its crater; there was Nautilus Bay, with False Hope Point projecting from it; and Deliverance Bay, protected by Shark's Island! And why should it not have been the guns from that battery whose report they had heard the day before, for there was no ship to be seen either in the bay or out in the open sea?

Joyful exceedingly, with throbbing hearts and eyes wet with tears of gratitude, all of them joined with Frank in the prayer which went up to God.

Chapter XI – By Well-Known Ways

The cave in which Mr. Wolston, Ernest, and Jack had spent the night four months before, on the day before the English flag was planted at the summit of Jean Zermatt peak, was that evening full of happiness. If no one enjoyed a tranquil sleep, sleeplessness was not due to bad dreams but to the excitement of the recent happenings.

After their prayer of thanksgiving, they had all declined to delay a minute longer at the summit of the peak. Not for two hours would day yield to night, and that time would be long enough for them to reach the foot of the range.

"It would be very strange," Fritz remarked, "if we could not find some cave large enough to shelter us all."

"Besides," Frank answered, "we shall be lying under the trees-under the trees of New Switzerland!New Switzerland!"

He could not refrain from saying the dear name over and over again, the name that was blessed by all.

"Speak it again, Dolly dear!" he exclaimed. "Say it again, that I may hear it once more."

"New Switzerland!" laughed the girl, her eyes shining with happiness.

"New Switzerland!" Jenny repeated, holding Fritz's hand in her own.

And there was not one of them, not even Bob, who did not echo it.

"Well, good people," said Captain Harry Gould, "if we have made up our minds to go down to the foot of the mountain we have no time to lose."

"What about eating?" John Block inquired. "And how are we to get food on the

way?"

"In forty-eight hours we shall be at Rock Castle," Frank declared.

"Besides," Fritz said, "isn't there any quantity of game on the plains of New Switzerland?"

"And how are you going to hunt it without guns?" Captain Gould inquired. "Clever as Fritz and Frank are, I hardly imagine that merely by pointing a stick..."

"Pooh!"Fritz answered. "Haven't we got legs? You'll see, captain! Before mid-day tomorrow we shall have real meat instead of that turtle stuff."

"We must not abuse the turtles, Fritz," said Jenny, "if only out of gratitude."

"You are quite right, wife, but let us be off! Bob doesn't want to stay here any longer; do you, Bob?"

"No, no," the child replied; "not if papa and mama are coming too."

"And to think," said the boatswain slily, "to think that down there, in the south, we have got a beautiful beach where turtles and mussels swarm-and a beautiful cave where there are provisions for several weeks-and in that cave a beautiful bed of sea-weed-and we are going to leave all that for..."

"We will come back for our treasures by and by!" Fritz promised.

"But still-" John Block persisted.

"Oh, shut up, you wretched fellow!" Captain Gould ordered, laughing.

"I'll shut up, captain; there are only two words more I should like to say."

"What are they?"

"Out away!"

As usual, Fritz took the lead. They descended the cone without any difficulty, and reached the foot of the range. Some happy instinct, a genuine sense of direction, had led them to take the same path as Mr. Wolston, Ernest, and Jack had taken, and it was barely eight o'clock when they reached the edge of the vast pine-forest.

And by a no less happy chance-there seemed nothing surprising in it, for they had entered upon the season of happy chances the boatswain found the cave in which Mr. Wolston and the two brothers had taken shelter. It was rather small, but large enough for Jenny and Dolly and

Susan and little Bob. The men could sleep in the open air. They could tell, from the white ashes of a fire, that the cave had been occupied before.

Perhaps all the members of the two families had crossed this forest and climbed the peak on which the British flag was waving!

After supper, when Bob had fallen asleep in a corner of the cave, they talked long, notwithstanding all the fatigue of the day, and the talk turned upon the *Flag*.

During the week that they had been held prisoners, the ship must have sailed northwards. The only explanation of that could be the persistence of contrary winds, for it was manifestly to the interest of Robert Borupt and the crew to reach the far waters of the Pacific. If they had not done so it was because the weather had prevented them.

Everything now went to show that the *Flag* had been driven towards the Indian Ocean, into the proximity of New Switzerland. Reckoning the time that had passed, and the course that had been followed, since the boat had been cast adrift, the incontestable conclusion followed that on that day Harry Gould and his companions could not have been much more than a couple of hundred miles from the desired island, though they had imagined themselves separated from it by a thousand or more.

The boat had touched land on the southern coast, which Fritz and Frank did not know at all, the other side of the mountain range which they had seen for the first time when they came out into the Green Valley. Who could have dreamed that there could be such an amazing difference in the nature of the soil and its products between the rich country to the north of the range and the arid plateau which extended from the peak to the sea?

Now they could understand the arrival of the albatross on the other side of the cliff. After Jenny Montrose's departure the bird had probably returned to Burning Rock, whence it flew sometimes to the shore of New Switzerland, though it had never gone either to Falconhurst or Rock Castle.

What a big part the faithful bird had played in their salvation! It was to him that they owed the discovery of that second cavern into which little Bob had followed him, and, as a consequence, the finding of the passage which came out on the top of the cliff.

The conversation lasted far into the night. But at last fatigue overcame them, and they slept. But at early dawn they took some food and set out again in high spirits.

Besides the traces of a fire in the cave, the little band encountered other signs in the forest and the open country. The trampled grass and broken branches were caused by the constant movement of animals, ruminants or beasts of prey, but it was impossible to be under any misapprehension when they came upon the traces of encampments.

"Besides," Fritz pointed out, "who but our own people could have planted the flag on the summit of that peak?"

"Unless it went and planted itself there!" the boatswain replied with a laugh.

"Which would not be a surprising thing for an English flag to do!" Fritz replied cheerfully.

"There are quite a lot of places where it would seem to have grown by itself!"

Led by Fritz, the party descended the first slopes of the range, which were partly covered by the forest.

Great obstacles to overcome or serious risks to be incurred seemed unlikely on the way from the range to the Promised Land.

The distance between the two points might be estimated at twenty miles. If they did ten miles a day, with a halt for two hours at midday, and slept one night on the way, they could reach the defile of Cluse in the evening of the following day.

From the defile to Rock Castle or to Falconburst would be a matter of a few hours only.

"Ah," said Frank, "if we only had our two good buffaloes, Storm and Grumbler, or Fritz's onager, or Whirlwind, Jack's ostrich. it would only take us one day to get to Rock Castle!"

"I am sure that Frank for got to post the letter we wrote, asking them to send the animals to us," Jenny answered merrily.

"What, Frank, did you forget?" asked Fritz. "A thoughtful, attentive fellow like you?"

"No," said Frank, "it was Jenny who forgot to tie a note to her albatross's leg before he flew off."

"How thoughtless of me!" the young woman exclaimed.

"But it is not certain that the postman would have taken the letter to the right address," Dolly said.

"Who knows?" Frank replied. "Everything that is happening now is so extraordinary."

"Well," said Captain Gould, "since we can't count upon Storm or Grumbler or Whirlwind or the onager, the best thing we can do is to trust to our own legs."

"And to step lively," John Block added. They started with the firm intention only to halt at mid-day. From time to time James and Frank and the boatswain carried Bob, although the child wanted to walk. So they lost no time crossing the forest.

James and Susan Wolston, who knew nothing of the marvels of New Switzerland, were filled with constant admiration of the luxuriant vegetation, which is far finer than that of Cape Colony.

And yet they were only in the part of the island which was left to itself, and had never been touched by the hand of man! What would it be like when they came to the cultivated portion of the district, to the farms at Eberfurt, Sugar-cane Grove, Wood Grange, and Prospect Hill, the rich territory of the Promised Land?

Game abounded everywhere-agoutis, peccaries, cavies, antelopes, and rabbits, besides bustards, partridges, grouse, hazel-hens, guinea fowls, and ducks. Fritz and Frank had good reason to regret not having their sporting guns with them. The cavies and peccaries and agoutis would not let anyone come near them, and it seemed likely that they would be reduced to finishing what was left of their provisions for their next meal.

But then the question of food was resolved by a stroke of luck.

About eleven o'clock, Fritz, walking in front, made a sign for everyone to stop at the edge of a little clearing crossed by a narrow stream, on the bank of which an animal was quenching its thirst.

111

It was an antelope, and it meant wholesome and refreshing meat if only they could contrive to capture it somehow!

The simplest plan seemed to be to make a ring around the clearing, without allowing themselves to be seen, and directly the antelope attempted to break out, to stop its way, regardless of danger from its horns, overpower, and kill it.

The difficulty was to carry through this operation without alarming an animal whose sight is so keen, hearing so sharp, and scent so delicate.

While Jenny and Susan and Dolly and Bob halted behind a bush, Fritz, Frank, James, Captain Gould, and the boatswain, armed only with their pocket knives, began to work round the clearing, keeping well under cover in the thickets.

The antelope went on drinking at the stream, showing no signs of uneasiness, until Fritz got up sharply and uttered a loud shout.

At once the animal sprang up, stretched out its neck, and jumped towards the brake, which it could have cleared in a single leap.

It made for the side where Frank and John Block were standing, each with knife in hand.

The beast sprang, but took off badly, fell back, bowled the boatswain over, and struggled to rise.

Then up came Fritz, and throwing himself upon the animal, succeeded in driving his knife into its flank. But this one blow would not have been sufficient if Captain Gould had not succeeded in cutting its throat.

The animal lay motionless among the branches, and the boatswain got up nimbly.

"Confounded brute!" exclaimed John Block, who had escaped with a few bruises.

"I've shipped more than one heavy sea in my time, but never been bowled over like that!"

"I hope you are not much hurt, Block!" Captain Gould asked.

"No, only scratched, and that don 't matter, captain. What annoys me is to have been turned upside down like that."

"Well, to make up for it we will keep the best bit for you," Jenny answered.

"No, Mrs. Fritz, no! no! I would rather have the bit that pitched me on to the ground. That was its head. I want that animal's head!"

They set to work to cut up the antelope and take out the edible parts. Since they were now assured of food to last them until the evening of the following day, there would be no need for them to trouble further about it before they got to the defile of Cluse.

Fritz and Frank were no novices where the preparation of game was concerned. Had they not studied it in theory and in practice in twelve years' hunting among the grass-lands and woods of the Promised Land? Nor was the boatswain clumsy over the job. He seemed to derive real revengeful pleasure in skinning the animal. Within a quarter of an hour the haunches, cutlets, and other savory portions were ready to be grilled over the embers.

As it was nearly noon, it seemed best to camp in the clearing, where the stream would furnish clear, fresh water. Captain Gould and James lighted a wood fire at the foot of a mangrove. Then Fritz placed the best bits of the antelope over the glowing embers and left Susan and Dolly to superintend the cooking.

By a lucky chance Jenny had just found a quantity of roots such as can be roasted in the ashes. They were of a kind to satisfy hungry stomachs, and would agreeably complete the bill of fare for luncheon.

No flesh is more delicate than that of the an tel ope, which is both fragrant and tender, and everybody agreed that this was a real treat.

"How good it is," John Block exclaimed, "to eat real meat which has walked in its lifetime, and not crawled clumsily over the ground!"

"We won't cry down turtles," Captain Gould replied; "not even to sing the praises of antelope."

"The captain is right," said Jenny. "Without those excellent creatures, which have fed us ever since we got to the island, what would have become of us?"

"Then here's luck to turtles!" cried the boatswain. "But give me another chop."

When this refreshing meal was finished, they set out once more. They had no time to lose if the afternoon stage was to complete the ten miles planned for the day.

If Fritz and Frank had been alone, they would have paid no heed to fatigue. They would have marched all night and made but a single stage of the whole journey to the defile. They may have had the idea now, and it was certainly very tempting, for they could have got to Rock Castle in the afternoon of the following day. But they did not venture to suggest going on ahead.

Besides, think of the happiness of all arriving together at their much-desired goal, to throw themselves into the arms of the relations and friends who had been waiting so long for them, who might have lost all hope of ever seeing them again!

The second stage was done under the same conditions as the first, in order to husband the strength of Jenny and Dolly and Susan Wolston.

No incident occurred, and about four o'clock in the afternoon the edge of the forest was reached.

A fertile champaign extended beyond. Its vegetation was entirely due to the productivity of the soil, verdant grass-lands and woods or clumps of trees studding the country right up to the entrance to the Green Valley.

A few herds of stags and deer passed in the distance, but there was no question of hunting them. Numerous flocks of ostriches were also seen, reminding Fritz and Frank of their expedition to the country near the Arabian Watch-tower.

Several elephants appeared as well. They moved quietly through the thick woods, and one could imagine the longing eyes with which Jack would have regarded them if he had been there!

"While we have been away," Fritz said, "Jack may have succeeded in capturing an elephant, and taming and training it, as we did Storm and Grumbler and Lightfoot!"

"It's quite possible, dear," Jenny answered. "After fourteen months' absence we must expect to find something new in New Switzerland."

"Our second fatherland!" Frank said.

"I am already picturing other houses there," Dolly exclaimed, "and other farms perhaps a village even!"

"Well," said the boatswain, "I could be quite content with what we see about us; and I can 't imagine anything better in your island than we have here."

"It is nothing compared with the Promised Land, Mr. Block," Dolly declared.

"Nothing," Jenny agreed. "M. Zermatt gave it that Bible name because it deserved it, and we, more blest than the children of Israel, are about to set foot in the land of Canaan."

And John Block admitted they were right.

At six o'clock they stopped for the night.

There was little likelihood of change in the weather at this season, and the cold was not formidable. Indeed, they had suffered rather from heat during the day, in spite of the fact that they were in the shelter of the trees during the hottest hours. After that, a few isolated woods and copses had enabled them to walk in the shade without wandering too far from the direct route.

Supper was prepared, as the earlier meal had been, before a crackling fire of dry wood. This night would not be spent within a cave, but, with fatigue to rock them, not one of them lay awake.

As a matter of precaution, however, Fritz and Frank and the boatswain decided to keep alternate watch. When darkness fell, roaring could be heard in the far distance. There were wild beasts in this part of the island.

Next morning a start was made at daybreak. They hoped to get through the defile of Cluse in the second stage of the journey, if they met with no obstacles on the way.

There were no more hardships about the march to-day than there had been the day before. They went from wood to wood, so to speak, avoiding as much as possible the rays of the sun.

After the mid-day meal, taken by the side of a fast-running river twenty to thirty yards in width, flowing towards the north, they merely had to go along the left bank.

Neither Fritz nor Frank knew this river, since their expeditions had never brought them into the heart of the island. They had no idea that it had already received a name, that it was called the Montrose, as they had no knowledge of the new name of Jean Zermatt peak, on whose summit the British flag was floating. What a pleasure it would be to Jenny to learn that this river bore the name of her family!

After marching for an hour they left the Montrose, which bore off sharply to the east. Two hours later Fritz and Frank, who had taken the lead, set foot at length on country known to them.

"The Green Valley!" they shouted, and saluted it with a cheer.

It was the Green Valley, and now they only had to get to the rampart enclosing the Promised Land to be at the defile of Cluse.

This time, no consideration, no hunger or fatigue, could have availed to hold back any of them. Following Fritz and Frank, they all hurried forward, although the path was steep. They seemed to be impelled forcibly towards the goal which they had despaired of ever attaining!

Oh, if only by some extraordinary good luck M. Zermatt and Mr. Wolston might be at the hermitage at Eberfurt, and their families with them, as the custom was during the summer season!

But that would have been too good to be true, as people say. Not even John Block dared to hope for it.

The beams across the entrance were all in place, fixed firmly between interstices among the rocks so as to resist the efforts of even the most powerful animals.

"That is our door!"Fritz cried.

"Yes," said Jenny, "the door into the Promised Land where all our dear ones live!"

They only had to remove one of the beams, a task which took but a few minutes.

And then at last they were through the defile, and all had the feeling that they were entering their own home-home, which, only three days ago, they had supposed to be hundreds and hundreds of miles away!

Fritz and Frank and John Block replaced the beam in its proper grooves so as to bar the way against wild beasts and pachyderms.

About half-past seven night was falling with the suddenness peculiar to the tropics when Fritz and his companions reached the hermitage

at Eberfurt.

Nobody was at the farm, and, although they regretted this, there was no occasion for them to be surprised.

The little villa was in perfect order. They opened all the doors and windows, and proceeded to make themselves comfortable for the ten hours or so they would stay.

In accordance with M. Zermatt's practice, the house was quite ready for the reception of the two families, who visited it several times in the course of the year. The bedsteads were given to Jenny and Dolly, Susan and little Bob, and to Captain Gould. Dry grass spread on the floor of the out-house would be good enough for the others this last night before their return home.

Moreover, Eberfurt was always provided with stores to last a week.

So Jenny only had the trouble of opening large wicker hampers, to find preserves of various kinds, sago, cassava, or tapioca flour, and salted meat and fish. As for fruit-figs, man goes, bananas, pears and apples-they only had to take a step to pick them from the trees, and only another to gather vegetables in the kitchen garden.

Of course the kitchen and larder were properly equipped with all necessary utensils. Directly a good wood fire was crackling in the stove, the pot was set upon its tripod. Water was drawn from an off-shoot from the Eastern River, which supplied the reservoir belonging to the farm. And it was with special pleasure that Fritz and Frank were able to offer their guests glasses of palm wine drawn from the barrels in the cellar.

"Ah-ha!" cried the boatswain. "We've been teetotallers a very long time. "

"Well, we will pledge you now, good old Block!" Fritz exclaimed.

"As much as you like," the boatswain answered. "Nothing could be more pleasant than drinking one another's health in this excellent wine."

"Let us drink then," said Frank, "to the happiness of seeing our parents and our friends again at Falconhurst or Rock Castle!"

And, clinking glasses, they gave three cheers for the Zermatts and the Wolstons.

"Seriously," John Block remarked, "there are plenty of inns in England and elsewhere which aren't nearly so good as this hermitage of Eberfurt."

"Moreover, Block," Fritz answered, "here the entertainment is free!"

When supper was finished all sought the repose of which they had such need after their long day's march.

Every one of them slept until the sun rose next morning.

Chapter XII – Enemies In The Promised Land

At seven o'clock next morning, after breakfasting off the remains of supper and drinking a stirrup-cup of palm wine, Fritz and his companions left the hermitage at Eberfurt.

They were all in haste, and intended to cover the seven and a half miles that lay between the farm and Falconhurst in less than three hours.

"It is possible that our people may be settled now in their dwelling in the air," Fritz remarked.

"If so, dear," said Jenny, "we shall have the joy of meeting them quite an hour sooner."

"Provided they have not gone into summer quarters on Prospect Hill," Frank observed. "In that case we should be obliged to go back to False Hope Point."

"Isn't that the cape from which M. Zermatt must watch for the *Unicorn?*" Captain Gould inquired.

"That is the one, captain," Fritz replied; "and as the corvette must have completed her repairs, it will not be long before she reaches the island."

"However that may be," the boatswain remarked, "the best thing we can do, in my opinion, is to start. If there is nobody at Falconhurst we will go to Rock Castle, and if there is nobody at Rock Castle we will go to Prospect Hill, or anywhere else. But let us get on the march!"

Although there was no lack of kitchen utensils and gardening tools at the hermitage, Fritz had looked in vain for any sporting guns and ammunition. When his father and brothers came to the farm they brought their guns, but never left them there. However, there was nothing to be afraid of in crossing the Promised Land, since no wild beasts could get through the defile of Cluse.

A cart road-and how often already had it been rolled by the wagon which the buffaloes and the onager drew!-ran between the cultivated fields, now in their full vegetation, and the woods in their full verdure. The sight of all this prosperity gladdened the eye. Captain Gould and the boatswain, and James and Susan Wolston, who saw this district for the first time, were amazed. Most certainly might colonists come here; it could support hundreds, the island as a whole could thousands!

After marching for an hour and a half, Fritz stopped for a few moments, nearly midway between the hermitage of Eberfurt and Falconhurst, before a stream which he did not know existed in this part of the district.

"That is something new," he said.

"It certainly is," Jenny answered. "I do not remember any stream in this place."

"It is more like a canal," Captain Gould remarked.

"You are right, captain," said Fritz. "Mr. Wolston must have conceived the idea of drawing water from Jackal River to supply Swan Lake and keep it full during the hot weather, which would enable them to irrigate the land round Wood Grange."

"Yes," Frank went on, "it must have been your father, Dolly, who had that notion and carried it out."

"Oh!" said Dolly. "But I expect your brother Ernest had a finger in the pie!"

"No doubt-our learned Ernest!" Fritz agreed.

"And why not the intrepid Jack-and M. Zermatt too?" Captain Gould inquired.

"Everybody, then," said Jenny, laughing. "Yes, every one of both the families, which now are really one," Fritz answered.

The boatswain broke in, as was his way, with a very just remark:

"If those who cut this canal did well, those who threw a bridge across it deserve quite as much praise. So let us go over and march on!"

They crossed the bridge and entered into the more thickly wooded district, where rose the little stream that ran out near Falconburst, just below Whale Island.

Fritz and Frank listened intently, trying to catch some distant sound of barking or of guns. What was Jack, the enthusiastic sportsman, about, that he was not hunting this fine morning? Game was rising in every direction, scampering away through the brakes and scattering from tree to tree. If the two brothers had had guns, they could have let fly with both barrels over and over again. It seemed to them that fur and feather had never been more plentiful in the district, so plentiful that their companions were genuinely astonished by it.

But, besides the twittering of little birds, the call of partridges and bustards, the chattering of parrots and sometimes the bowling of jackals were all that could be heard, and to these sounds was never added the report of fire-arms or the whimper of a dog on the scent.

After crossing the Falconhurst river they only had to go up the right bank as far as the edge of the wood, where grew the gigantic mangrove tree with the aerial dwelling-place.

A profound silence reigned underneath these immense trees-a silence which awakened vague uneasiness. When Fritz looked at Jenny he read in her eyes an anxiety for which, however, there was no justification as yet. Frank, too, felt some nervousness, walking on in front and then retracing his steps. This uneasiness was shared by all. In ten minutes they would be at Falconhurst. Ten minutes! Was not that much the same as being there already?

"It's a sure thing," said the boatswain, who wanted to cheer them up, "it's a sure thing that we shall have to go down this fine avenue of yours to Rock Castle! A delay of an hour, that's all. And what's an hour, after so long an absence?"

They put on pace. A few moments later they came within sight of the edge of the wood, and then of the enormous mangrove tree in the middle of the court-yard, enclosed by palisades fringed with a quickset hedge.

Fritz and Frank ran to the gate contrived in the hedge.

The gate was open, and had been torn half off its hinges.

The two brothers went into the court-yard and stopped beside the little central basin.

The place was deserted.

Not a sound came from the poultry run or the sheds built against the palisade, although these were generally full of cows and sheep and poultry during the summer season. In the out-houses were various things, boxes and hampers and agricultural implements, all in a disorder very foreign to the careful habits of Mme. Zermatt and Mrs. Wolston and her daughter.

Frank ran to the cattle-sheds.

There was nothing in them but a few armfuls of hay in the racks.

Did it mean that the animals had broken out of the enclosure? Were they straying loose about the country? No; for not one had been seen anywhere near Falconhurst. It was just possible that, for some reason or other, they had been penned in the other farms, and yet that was hardly an explanation.

As has been said, the farmstead of Falconburst comprised two dwelling-places, one built among the branches of the mangrove tree, the other among the roots which were buttressed round its base. Above the latter was a terrace with a railing of bamboo canes, which supported the roof of tarred moss. This terrace covered several rooms, divided by partitions fixed among the roots, and large enough for both families to inhabit them together. This first dwelling was as silent as the outbuildings in the yard.

"Let us go inside!" said Fritz, with trouble in his voice.

All followed him, and a cry broke from them-an inarticulate cry, for not one of them could have uttered a word.

The furniture was upset. The chairs and tables had been thrown down, the chests opened, the bedding thrown on the floor, the utensils into the corners. It was as if the rooms had been given over to pillage for the mere sake of pillage. Of the stores of provisions, generally kept fully supplied at Falconhurst, not a scrap remained. There was no hay in the loft; in the cellar the casks of wine and beer and spirits were empty. There were no weapons, except one loaded pistol which the boatswain picked up and thrust in his belt. Yet carbines and guns were always left at Falconhurst during the hunting season. Fritz, Frank, and Jenny stood overwhelmed before this most unexpected disaster. Were things in the same state at Rock Castle and Wood Grange, and Sugar-cane Grove

122

and Prospect Hill? Of all the farms, had the hermitage of Eberfurt alone been spared by these pillagers! And who were the pillagers?

"My friends," said Captain Gould, "some disaster has happened; but it may not be as serious as you fear."

No one answered. What answer could Fritz or Frank or Jenny have given? Their hearts seemed broken. They had set foot within the Promised Land with so much joy, only to find ruin and desolation!

But what had happened? Had New Switzerland been invaded by a band of those pirates who were so numerous at that period in the Indian Ocean, where the Andamans and Nicobars offered them a safe place of refuge? Had the Zermatts and Wolstons been able to leave Rock Castle in time, and retire elsewhere, or even flee from the island? Had they fallen into the hands of the pirates-or had they lost their lives in an attempt at self-defense?

And, one last question, had all this happened a few months ago, or a few weeks ago, or a few days ago, and would it have been possible to prevent it if the *Unicorn* had arrived within the time arranged?

Jenny made a brave effort to keep back her tears, while Susan and Dolly sobbed together. Frank wanted to rush to find his father and mother and brothers, and Fritz was obliged to hold him back. Captain Gould and the boatswain went out several times to examine the ground near the palisade, but came back without having found anything to throw light on the matter.

Some decision, however, had to be arrived at. Was it better to remain at Falconhurst and await events there, or to go down to Rock Castle ignorant of bow matters stood? Should they make a reconnaissance, leaving the women and Bob in James' protection, while Fritz, Frank, and Captain Gould, and John Block went to investigate either along the shore or across country?

In any case they had to dispel this uncertainty, even though the truth should leave them without hope!

Fritz was voicing the general wish when he said:

"Let us try to get to Rock Castle."

"And let us go at once!" Frank exclaimed.

"I will come with you," said Captain Gould.

"And so will I," said John Block.

"Good!" Fritz replied. "But James must stay with Jenny, Dolly, and Susan, who will be out of harm's way at the top of Falconburst."

"Let us all go up first," John Block suggested, "and from there, perhaps, we shall see."

It was only reasonable to do that before going to reconnoitre outside. From the aerial dwelling-place, and especially from the top of the mangrove tree, the view extended over much of the Promised Land and the sea to the east, and also over nearly eight miles of coast between Deliverance Bay and False Hope Point.

"Up! Up!" Fritz answered, to the boatswain's suggestion.

The habitation among the branches of the tree had escaped the general devastation, thanks to the dense foliage of the mangrove, which almost concealed it from view. The door giving access to the winding staircase inside the trunk bore no marks of violence. Frank found it shut, and wrenched at it so that the lock-bolt came away.

In a few moments they had all climbed up the staircase, lighted by narrow loopholes in the tree, and set foot on the circular balcony, which was almost completely screened behind a curtain of leaves.

The instant Fritz and Frank reached the platform they hurried into the first room.

Neither this room nor the rooms next it presented the least sign of disturbance. The bedding was all in good condition, the furniture all in place. So it was obvious that the original Falcon's nest had been respected. The marauders could not have found the door below. The foliage had become so very much thicker in the course of these twelve years that it would have been as impossible to see the dwelling from the yard below as it was from the edge of the neighboring wood.

It really looked as if Mme. Zermatt and Mrs. Wolston had set everything in order only the day before. There were preserved meat, flour, rice, preserves, and liquor, enough of everything to last for a week, in accordance with the usual custom observed at Falconhurst as at the other farms.

The Castaways of the Flag

Nobody now, of course, gave a thought to the question of food. What occupied their minds to the exclusion of all else, filling them with despair, was the deserted condition of Falconhurst in the height of the summer, and the pillage of the lower dwelling.

Directly they returned to the balcony Fritz and the boatswain clambered up to the top of the mangrove tree, to get as wide a view as possible.

To north ran the line of coast bounded by False Hope Point at the little hill where the villa of Prospect Hill stood. Nothing suspicious could be detected in this part of the district.

To west, beyond the canal connecting Jackal River with Swan Lake, spread the country watered by the little Falconhurst river, through which Fritz and his companions had walked after they had crossed the bridge. This was as deserted as the country which ran still further to the west as far as the defile of Cluse.

To east, the vast arm of the sea spread out between False Hope Point and Cape East, behind which lay Unicorn Bay. There was not a sail to be seen at sea, not a boat along the shore. Nothing was visible but the vast plain of water, from which, to north-east, projected, the reef upon which the *Landlord* had struck long ago.

Turning towards the south, the eye could only see, about two miles and a half away, the entrance into Deliverance Bay, near the wall of rock which sheltered the dwelling of Rock Castle.

Of that house, and its annexes, nothing was visible except the green tops of the trees in the kitchen garden, and, a little more to southwest, a line of light which indicated the course of Jackal River.

Fritz and John Block came down to the balcony again, after spending some ten minutes in the first examination. Making use of the telescope which M. Zermatt always kept at Falconburst, they had looked carefully in the direction of Rock Castle and the shore.

No one was to be seen there. It seemed that the two families could not be on the island now.

But it was possible that M. Zermatt and his people had been led by the marauders to some farmstead in the Promised Land, or even to some other part of New Switzerland.

To this suggestion, however, Captain Gould raised an objection which it was difficult to meet.

"These marauders, whoever they may be," he said, "must have come by sea: must even have landed in Deliverance Bay. Now we have observed none of their boats. The conclusion would seem to be that they have gone away again-perhaps taking-"

He stopped. No one ventured to make answer.

Certainly Rock Castle did not seem to be inhabited now. From the top of the tree no smoke could be seen rising above the fruit trees in the kitchen garden.

Captain Gould then suggested that the two families might have left New Switzerland voluntarily, since the *Unicorn* had not arrived at the appointed time.

"How could they have gone?" Fritz asked, who would have been glad to have this hope to cling to.

"Aboard some ship that came to these waters," Captain Gould replied; "one of the ships which must have been sent from England or perhaps another vessel which arrived off the island in the ordinary chances of navigation."

This theory was possible. And yet there were many grave reasons to suppose that the desertion of New Switzerland was not due to any such circumstance.

Fritz spoke again.

"We must not hesitate any longer. Let us go and look!"

"Yes, let us go!" said Frank.

Fritz was just preparing to go down again when Jenny stopped him.

"Smoke!" she said. "I think I can see smoke rising above Rock Castle."

Fritz seized the telescope and turned it towards the south; for more than a minute his eye stayed glued to the instrument.

Jenny was right. Smoke was passing across the curtain of green, above the rocks which enclosed Rock Castle to the rear.

The Castaways of the Flag

"They are there! They are there!" cried Frank. "And we ought to have been with them already!"

This assertion nobody denied. They all had such dire need to recover hope that everything was forgotten, the solitude that lay round Falconhurst, the pillage of the yard, the absence of the domestic animals, the empty sheds, the ruin of the rooms at the foot of the mangrove tree.

But cold reason came back, to Captain Gould and John Block at least. Manifestly Rock Castle was occupied at this moment-the smoke proved that. But might it not be occupied by the marauders? At any rate, it would be necessary to approach it with the utmost caution. Perhaps it would be best not to go along the avenue which led to Jackal River.

If they went across fields, and, as much as possible, from wood to wood, they might have a chance of getting to the drawbridge without being sighted.

At last, as ail were getting ready to leave the aerial dwelling, Jenny lowered the telescope, with which she had been scanning the coast of the bay.

"And the proof that both families are still here," she said, "is that the flag is flying over Shark's Island."

The white and red flag, the colors of New Switzerland, was indeed waving over the battery.

But did that make it absolutely certain that M. Zermatt and Mr. Wolston, and their wives and children, had not left the island? Did not the flag always float at that spot?

They would not argue the point. Everything would be explained at Rock Castle, and before an hour had passed.

"Let us go! Let us go!" said Frank a gain, and he turned towards the staircase.

"Stop! Stop!" the boatswain suddenly said, lowering his voice.

They watched him crawl along the balcony, to the side overlooking Deliverance Bay. Then he moved the leaves aside, put his head through them and drew it back precipitately.

"What is the matter?" Fritz asked.

"Savages!" John Block replied.

Chapter XIII – Shark's Island

It was now half-past two in the afternoon. The foliage of the mangrove was so dense that the rays of the sun, though almost vertical, could not penetrate it. Thus Fritz and his companions ran no risk of being detected in the aerial dwelling of Falconhurst, of the existence of which the savages who had landed on the island had no idea.

Five men, half naked, with the black skins of natives of Western Australia, armed with bows and arrows, were coming along the path. They had no notion that they had been seen, or even that there were other inhabitants of the Promised Land besides those of Rock Castle.

But what had become of M. Zermatt and the others? Had they been able to make their escape? Had they fallen in unequal combat?

Of course, as John Block remarked, it could not be supposed that the number of aborigines who had landed on the island was limited to these few men. Had they been so inferior numerically, they could not have got the better of M. Zermatt and his two sons and Mr. Wolston, even if they had made a surprise attack. It must have been a large band that had invaded New Switzerland, whither they must have come in a fleet of canoes. The fleet was doubtless lying at the present moment in the creek, with the boat and the pinnace. It could not be seen from the top of Falconhurst because the view in that direction was cut off by the point of Deliverance Bay.

And where were the Zermatts and the Wolstons? What inference must be drawn from the fact that they had not been encountered at Falconhurst or thereabouts?

That they were prisoners at Rock Castle, that they had had neither time nor opportunity to seek refuge in the other farms-or that they had been massacred?

Everything else was explained now-the havoc wrought at Falconhurst, and the deserted condition in which the Promised Land was found between the Swan Lake canal and the shore.

How could they cherish any but the faintest hope? So, while Captain Gould and the boatswain kept the natives in view, the others sorrowed together.

There was one last chance. Could the two families have taken refuge in the westward, in some part of the island beyond Pearl Bay? If they had caught sight of the canoes in the distance, across Deliverance Bay, might they not have had time to make their escape in the wagon, taking provisions and arms?

Captain Gould and John Block continued to watch the approaching savages.

Was it their intention to come into the yard? The house had been visited and pillaged by them already. Now they might discover the door at the foot of the staircase. In that event, however, they could easily be disposed of. For when they stepped out on to the platform they could be surprised, one by one, and hurled over the balustrade, a drop of forty or fifty feet.

"And," as the boatswain remarked, "if after a tumble like that they had legs enough left to get to Rock Castle, the beasts would be more like cats than the monkeys they resemble!"

But when they reached the end of the avenue, the five men stopped. The watchers did not miss a single movement they made. What was their business at Falconhurst? If the aerial dwelling had escaped their observation so far, were they not now on the point of discovering it, and the people inside it? And then, they would come back in larger numbers, and how was the attack of a hundred natives to be withstood?

They came to the palisade and walked all round it. Three of them entered the yard, and went into one of the out-houses on the left, coming out again presently with fishing tackle.

"The rascals are a bit too familiar!" the boatswain murmured. "They don't only not ask your leave—"

"Can they have a canoe on the beach, and are they going to fish along the shore?" said Captain Gould.

"We'll soon find out, Skipper," John Block replied.

The three men returned to their companions. Then they went down a little path bordered with a stout thorn hedge, which ran along the right of the Falconhurst river and passed on to the sea.

130

They were in sight until they reached the cutting through which the river flowed to its outlet into Flamingo Bay.

But as soon as they turned to the left, they became invisible, and would only be seen again if they put out to sea. It was probable there was a boat upon the beach-probable, too, that they generally used it for fishing near Falconburst. While Captain Gould and John Block remained on the watch, Jenny controlled her grief and asked Fritz:

"What ought we to do, dear?"

Fritz looked at his wife, not knowing what to answer.

"We are going to decide what we ought to do," Captain Gould declared. "But to begin with, it is idle to remain on this balcony, where we are in danger of being discovered."

When they were all together in the room, while Bob, who was tired by his long march, slept in a little closet next to it, Fritz answered his wife's question:

"No, Jenny dear-all hope is not lost of finding our people. It is possible that they were not taken by surprise. Father and Mr. Wolston are sure to have seen the canoes in the distance. They may have had time to take refuge in one of the farms, or even in the heart of the woods at Pearl Bay, where these savages would not have ventured. We saw no trace of them when we left the hermitage at Eberfurt, after we crossed the canal. My opinion is that they have not moved away from the coast."

"That is my opinion, too," said Captain Gould, "and I believe that M. Zermatt and Mr. Wolston have got away with their families."

"Yes, I am sure of it!" said Jenny positively. "Dolly, dear-Susan-don't lose heart! Don 't cry any more! We shall see them all again!"

The young woman spoke so stoutly that she brought back hope to them. Fritz shook her hand.

"It is God who speaks through your lips, Jenny dear!" he said.

On consideration, indeed, as Captain Gould insisted, it was hardly to be supposed that Rock Castle could have been surprised by attacking natives, for they could not have brought their canoes by night to land which they did not know. It must have been by daylight that they arrived, and some of the islanders must surely have seen them far enough off to have had time to take refuge in some other part of the island.

"And then again," Fritz added, "if these natives landed only recently, our people may not have been at Rock Castle at all. This is the season when we usually visit all the farms. Although we did not meet them at the hermitage at Eberfurt last night, they may be at Wood Grange, or Prospect Hill, or at Sugarcane Grove, in the midst of those thick woods."

"Let us go to Sugar-cane Grove first," Frank suggested.

"We can do that," John Block assented; "but not before night."

"Yes, now, at once, at once!" Frank insisted, declining to listen to argument. "I can go alone. About twelve miles there, and twelve miles back; I shall be back in four hours, and we shall know what we are about."

"No, Frank, no!" said Fritz. "I do beg you not to leave us. It would be most foolish. If need be, I order you not to, and I am your elder brother."

"Would you stop me, Fritz?"

"I would deter you from doing anything so rash."

"Frank, Frank!" said Dolly entreatingly.

"Do please listen to your brother! Frank! I beseech you!"

But Frank was set on his plan.

"Very well!" said the boatswain, who thought it his duty to interfere. "Since a search is to be made, let us make it without waiting until night. But why should we not all go together to Sugar-cane Grove?"

"Then come along!" said Frank.

"But," the boatswain went on, addressing Fritz, "is it really Sugar-cane Grove that we ought to make for?"

"Where else?"Fritz asked.

The Castaways of the Flag

"Rock Castle!" John Block answered.

The name, thus unexpectedly dropped into the discussion, altered the whole course of it.

Rock Castle? After all, if M. Zermatt and Mr. Wolston and their wives and children had fallen into the hands of the natives, and if their lives had been spared, it was there that they would be, for the smoke proved that Rock Castle was occupied.

"Go to Rock Castle, eh?" Captain Gould replied. "All right; but go there all together."

"All together?"

"No," said Fritz; "only two or three of us, and after dark."

"After dark." Frank began again, more set than ever upon his idea. "I am going to Rock Castle now."

"And how do you expect in broad daylight to escape the savages who are prowling round about it?" Fritz replied. "And if you do escape them, how will you get into Rock Castle, if they are there at the time?"

"I don 't know, Fritz. But I shall find out if our people are there, and when I have found out I will come back!"

"My dear Frank," Captain Gould said, "I quite understand your impatience, and I sympathize with it. But do give way to us in this matter; it is only common prudence that makes us think as we do. If the savages get you, the hunt will be up; they will come to look for us, and there won 't be any more safety for us, either at Wood Grange or anywhere else."

At last they succeeded in making Frank listen to reason. He had to bow to the authority of one who already perhaps was the head of the family.

So it was decided that they should wait, and that as soon as darkness permitted Frank and the boatswain should leave Falconhurst. It was better that two should make this reconnaissance, fraught with many dangers. They would glide along the quickset hedge that bordered the avenue, and both would try to get to Jackal River. If the drawbridge were withdrawn to the other bank, they would swim across the river

133

and attempt to get into the court-yard of Rock Castle through the orchard. It would be easy to see through one of the windows if the families were shut up inside. If they were not, Frank and John Block would come back at once to Falconhurst, and they would all try to get to Sugar-cane Grove before daylight.

Never did the hours drag by more slowly! Never had Captain Gould and his companions been more profoundly dejected-not even when the boat was cast adrift upon an unknown sea, not even when it was smashed upon the rocks in Turtle Bay, not even when the shipwrecked company, with three women and a child amongst them, saw themselves threatened by winter on a desert coast, shut in a prison whence they could not escape!

In the midst of all those trials they had, at least, been free from anxiety on account of those in New Switzerland! Whereas, now, they had found the island in the power of a horde of natives, and did not know what had become of their relatives and friends; but had good ground for fearing that they might all have perished in a massacre!

Slowly the day wore on. Every now and then one or other of them, generally Fritz and the boatswain, climbed up among the branches of the mangrove in order to search the country and the sea. What they were most anxious to ascertain was whether the savages were still in the neighborhood of Falconhurst, or had gone back to Rock Castle.

But they could see nothing, except, towards the south, near the mouth of Jackal River, the little column of smoke rising above the rocks.

Up to four o'clock in the afternoon nothing happened to change the situation. A meal was prepared from the stores in the house. When Frank and John Block came back they might all have to set out for Sugar-cane Grove, and that would be a long march.

Suddenly a report was heard.

"What is that?" Jenny exclaimed, and Fritz drew her back as she was hastening to one of the windows.

"Could it have been a gun?" Frank asked.

"It was a gun!"the boatswain exclaimed.

"But who fired it?" Fritz said.

The Castaways of the Flag

"A ship off the island, do you think?" James suggested.

"The *Unicorn,* perhaps!" Jenny cried. "Then she must be very near the island."

John Block remarked, "for that report was close at hand."

"Come to the balcony, come to the balcony!" Frank cried excitedly.

"Let us be careful not to be seen, for the savages must be on the alert," Captain Gould cautioned them.

All eyes were turned towards the sea.

No ship was to be seen, although, judging from the nearness of the report, it must have been off Whale Island. All that the boatswain could see was a single canoe, manned by two men, which was trying to get in from the open sea to the beach at Falconhurst.

"Can they be Ernest and Jack?" Jenny whispered.

"No," Fritz answered, "those two men are natives, and the canoe is a pirogue."

"But why are they running away like that?" Frank asked. "Can there be someone after them?"

Fritz uttered a cry-a cry of joy and surprise combined.

He had just seen a bright flash in the middle of a white smoke, and almost simultaneously there was a second report which made the echoes ring round the coast.

At the same time a ball, skimming the surface of the bay, threw up a great jet of water a couple of fathoms away from the canoe, which continued to fly at full speed towards Falconburst.

"There! There!" shouted Fritz. "Father and Mr. Wolston and all of them are there on Shark's Island!"

It was, indeed, from that island that the first report had come, as well as the second with the ball aimed at the pirogue. No doubt the islanders had found refuge under the protection of the battery which the savages did not venture to approach. Above it was the red and white flag of New Switzerland, while on the topmost peak in all the island floated the British flag!

Impossible to depict the joy, the delirium to which those so lately in despair now abandoned themselves! And their emotions were shared by those true comrades, Captain Gould and the boatswain.

There was no further idea of going to Rock Castle; they would leave Falconhurst only to go-how, they did not know-to Shark's Island. If only it had been possible to communicate with it by signals from the top of the mangrove, to wave a flag to which the flag on the battery might reply! But that might have been unwise, unwise too, to fire a few shots with the pistol, for, though these might be heard by M. Zermatt, they might also be heard by the savages, if they were still prowling about Falconhurst.

It was most important that they should not know of the presence of Captain Gould and his party, for these could not have withstood a combined attack by all the savages now in possession of Rock Castle.

"Our position is a good one now," Fritz remarked; "don't let us do anything to compromise it."

"Quite so," Captain Gould replied. "Since we have not been discovered, don't let us run any risk of it. Let us wait until night before we do anything."

"How will it be possible to get to Shark's Island?" Jenny asked.

"By swimming," Fritz declared. "Yes; I can swim there all right. And since father must have fled there in the long boat, I will bring back the long boat to take you all over."

"Fritz,-dear!" Jenny could not refrain from protesting." Swim across that arm of the sea?"

"Mere sport for me, dear wife, mere sport!" the intrepid fellow answered.

"Perhaps the niggers' canoe is still upon the beach," John Block suggested.

Evening drew on, and a little after seven o'clock it was dark, for night follows day with hardly any interval of twilight in these latitudes.

About eight o'clock the time had come, and it was arranged that Fritz and Frank and the boatswain should go down into the yard. They were to satisfy themselves that the natives were not hanging about anywhere near, and then were to venture down to the shore. In any case, Captain Gould, James Wolston, Jenny, Dolly and Susan were to wait at the foot of the tree for a signal to join them.

So the three crept down the staircase. They had not dared to light a lantern lest its light should betray them.

There was no one in the house below, nor in the out-houses. What had to be found out now was whether the men who had come during the day had gone back to Rock Castle, or if they were on the beach for which the canoe had made.

Caution was still necessary. Fritz and John Block decided to go down to the shore by themselves, while Frank remained on guard near the entrance to the yard, ready to run in if any danger threatened Falconhurst.

The two men went out of the palisade and crossed the clearing. Then they slid from tree to tree for a couple of hundred yards, listening, and peering, until they reached the narrow cutting between the last rocks, against which the waves broke.

The beach was deserted, and so was the sea as far as the cape, the outlines of which could just be seen in the eastward. There were no lights either in the direction of Rock Castle, or on the surface of Deliverance Bay. A single mass of rock loomed up a couple of miles out at sea.

It was Shark's Island.

"Come on," said Fritz.

"Ay, ay," John Block replied.

They went down to the sandy shore, whence the tide was receding.

They would have shouted for joy if they had dared. A canoe was there, lying on its side.

It was the pirogue which the battery had greeted with a couple of shots from its guns.

"A lucky thing that they missed it!" John Block exclaimed. "If they hadn't, it would be at the bottom now. If it was Mr. Jack or Mr. Ernest who was such a bad shot, we will offer him our congratulations!"

This little boat, of native construction and worked by paddles, could only hold five or six people. Captain Gould and his party numbered eight, and a child, to be rowed to Shark's Island. True, the distance was only a bare two miles.

"Well, we will pack in somehow," John Block said; "we mustn't have to make two trips."

"Besides," Fritz added, "in another hour the flood tide will make itself felt, and as it sets towards Deliverance Bay, not very far from Shark's Island, it will not be a very big job for us to get there."

"Everything is for the best," the boatswain replied, "and that is beginning to become evident."

There was no question of pushing the boat down to the sea; it would take the water of its own accord, directly the flood tide overtook it. John Block satisfied himself that it was firmly moored and was in no danger of drifting out to sea.

Then both went up the beach again into the avenue, and rejoined Frank, who was waiting for them in the court-yard.

Informed of what they had found, he was overjoyed. Fritz left him with the boatswain to keep watch over the entrances to the yard.

The news he brought made joy upstairs.

About half past nine all went down to the foot of the mangrove tree.

Frank and John Block had seen nothing suspicions. Silence reigned round Falconhurst. The slightest sound could have been heard, for there was not a breath of air.

With Fritz and Frank and Captain Gould in front, they crossed the court-yard and the clearing, and filing under cover of the trees in the a venue they reached the beach.

It was as deserted as it had been two hours before.

The Castaways of the Flag

The flood tide had already lifted the boat, which was floating at the end of its rope. Nothing now remained but to get into it, unmoor it, and push off into the current.

Jenny, Dolly, Susan, and the child immediately took their places in the stern. The others crouched between the seats, and Fritz and Frank took the paddles.

It was just ten o'clock, and, as there was no moon, they hoped they might get across unseen.

In spite of the great darkness, they would have no difficulty in making straight for the island.

The moment the pirogue was caught by the current it was carried towards it.

All kept silence. Not a word was exchanged, even under breath. Every heart was gripped by excitement.

The flood tide could not be relied upon to take them straight to Shark's Island. About a mile from the shore it bore away towards the mouth of Jackal River, to run up Deliverance Bay.

So Fritz and Frank paddled vigorously towards the dark mass of rock, where no sound or light could be detected.

But someone would certainly be on guard within the battery. Was there not a danger of the canoe being seen and shot at, under the misapprehension that the savages were making an attempt to get possession of the island under cover of the night?

Actually, the boat was not more than five or six cables' length away when a light flashed out at the spot where the guns stood under their shed.

Was it the flash from a gun? Was the air about to be rent by an explosion?

And then, caring no longer whether the savages heard him or not, the boatswain stood up and shouted in stentorian tones:

"Don't shoot! Don't shoot!"

"Friends-we are friends!" shouted Captain Gould.

Jules Verne

And Fritz and Frank together called again and yet again:

"It's we! It's we! It's we!"

The instant they touched the rocks they fell into the arms of their friends.

Chapter XIV – A Perilous Plight

A few minutes later the two families complete this time-with Captain Harry Gould and the boatswain, were together in the store-house in the middle of the island, five hundred paces from the battery knoll over which the flag of New Switzerland floated.

Fritz, Frank, and Jenny were clasped to the hearts of M. and Mme. Zermatt and covered with kisses; James, Dolly, Susan, and Bob were unable to extricate themselves from the embraces of Mr. and Mrs. Wolston; and much hand-shaking was exchanged with Captain Gould and the boatswain.

Then they had to exchange stories of the fifteen months which had passed since the day when the *Unicorn* disappeared behind the heights of False Hope Point, bearing away Jenny Montrose, Fritz, Frank, and Dolly.

But before recalling all these past events, it was necessary to talk of the present.

For although they were reunited now, the two families were none the less in a serious and perilous position. The savages must ultimately become masters of this island when the ammunition and provisions were exhausted, unless help came. And whence could M. Zermatt and his people expect help?

First of all Fritz told briefly the story of the *Flag's* castaways.

"And where are the savages?" Fritz asked, as he came to the end of telling how they had seen the savages.

"At Rock Castle," M. Zermatt replied.

"Many of them?"

"A hundred at least; they came in fifteen pirogues-probably from the Australian coast."

"Thank God you were able to escape from them!" Jenny exclaimed.

"Yes, indeed, dear child," M. Zermatt replied. "As soon as we saw the canoes making for Deliverance Bay, we took refuge on Shark's Island, thinking that we might be able to defend ourselves here against an attack by them."

"Papa," said Frank, "the savages know now that you are on this island."

"Yes, they do," M. Zermatt answered, "but thank God, they have not succeeded in landing here yet, and our old flag is still flying!"

The following is a very brief summary of what had happened since the time at which the first part of this narrative ended.

On the return of the dry season, after the expeditions which resulted in the discovery of the Montrose River, a reconnaissance was carried out as far as the range of mountains, where Mr. Wolston, Ernest and Jack planted the British flag on the summit of Jean Zermatt peak. That happened some ten or twelve days before the boat arrived on the southern coast of the island, and if the expedition had been carried beyond the range they might have met Captain Gould at Turtle Bay. But Mr. Wolston and the two brothers had not ventured across the desert plateau.

The new corners were told how Jack, carried away by his wild desire to capture a young elephant, had fallen into the midst of savages, who made him prisoner. After escaping from them, he had brought back the grave news of their presence on the island.

Thoroughly alarmed, the Zermatts and Wolstons made plans in anticipation of an attack upon Rock Castle, and maintained a watch day and night.

For three months, however, nothing happened. The savages did not appear. It seemed that they had finally left the island.

But there was matter of new anxiety in the fact that the *Unicorn,* due to arrive in September or October, made no appearance off New Switzerland. In vain did Jack go many times to the top of Prospect Hill to look out for the return of the corvette. On each occasion he had to come back to Rock Castle without having seen her.

It should be mentioned here that the ship observed by Mr. Wolston, Ernest, and Jack from the summit of Jean Zermatt peak was no other than the *Flag,* as could be proved by comparison of dates. Yes, it was the three-master which had fallen into the hands of Robert Borupt.

The Castaways of the Flag

After approaching the island, she had sailed to the Pacific Ocean, through the Sunda Seas, never to be heard of again.

The last weeks of the year brought them to despair. After the lapse of fifteen months, all abandoned hope of ever seeing the *Unicorn* again. Mme. Zermatt, Mrs. Wolston, and Hannah mourned their lost ones. None had courage left for anything. Nothing seemed of any use.

It was only after this long delay, that they took it for granted that the *Unicorn* had been wrecked, lost with all hands, and that nothing more would ever be heard of her, either in England or in the Promised Land!

For if the corvette had accomplished her outward voyage without mishap, after a call at the Cape of Good Hope lasting a few days, she would have reached Portsmouth, her destination, within three months. From there, a few months later, she would have sailed for New Switzerland, and several emigrant ships would have been dispatched soon after her to the English colony. The fact that no ship had visited this portion of the Indian Ocean meant that the *Unicorn* had foundered in the dangerous seas that lie between Australia and Africa before she had reached her first port of call, Cape Town; it meant, too, that the existence of the island was still unknown, and would remain unknown, unless the chances of navigation brought some other ship into these remote seas which, at this period, lay within none of the maritime routes.

During the first half of the dry season neither M. Zermatt nor Mr. Wolston thought of leaving Rock Castle. As a rule they spent the finest part of the year at Falconhurst, reserving a week each for the farms at Wood Grange, Sugar-cane Grove, Prospect Hill, and the hermitage at Eberfurt. On this occasion they limited themselves to the brief visits necessitated by their duty to the animals. They made no attempt to explore the other portions of the island outside the district of the Promised Land. Jack contented himself with hunting in the immediate neighborhood of Rock Castle, leaving Whirlwind and Storm and Grumbler idle. Various works which Mr. Wolston had planned to do, to which his engineering instinct had moved him, were left unattempted.

What was the use? In those four little words was summed up a volume of despondency.

So when they came to celebrate the festival of Christmas-kept with joy so many years-tears were in the eyes of all, and prayers rose for those who were not with them!

Thus the year 1817 opened. In that splendid summer season Nature was more lavish with her gifts than she had ever been before. But her generosity far exceeded the requirements of seven persons. The great house seemed empty, now that those they had expected could be looked for no longer!

And yet there came at times faint hopes that everything was not lost irreparably. Could the delay of the *Unicorn* be explained in no other way than by shipwreck with loss of all hands? Perhaps she had prolonged her stay in Europe. Perhaps quite soon they would see her topsails on the horizon, and the long pennon streaming from her mainmast.

It was in the second week of January of this most gloomy year that M. Zermatt saw a flotilla of pirogues round Cape East, and making for Deliverance Bay. Their appearance caused no great surprise, for after Jack had fallen into their hands, the savages could no longer be unaware that the island was inhabited.

In less than two hours the tide would bring the pirogues to the mouth of Jackal River. Manned by something like a hundred men, for, of course, the whole party that had landed on the island must have joined in this expedition, how would it be possible to offer them serious resistance?

Would it be well to take refuge at Falconburst, Wood Grange, Prospect Hill, Sugarcane Grove, or even at the hermitage at Eberfurt? Would they be any safer there? As soon as they had set foot on this rich domain of the Promised Land, the invaders would be sure to go all over it! Ought they to seek a more secret shelter in the unknown regions of the island, and would there be any certainty that they would not be discovered even there?

Then Mr. Wolston suggested that they should abandon Rock Castle in favor of Shark's Island. If they put off in the long boat behind the point of Deliverance Bay, and went along the Falconhurst shore, they might perhaps be able to get to the island before the pirogues arrived. There, at any rate, under the protection of the two cannon in the battery, they might defend themselves, if the natives attempted to set foot on the island.

Besides, if there were not time to take over the stores and provisions needed for a long stay, the store-house had beds and could accommodate the two families. The boat could be laden with articles of prime necessity. And further, as has been related before, Shark's Island had been planted with mangroves, palms, and other trees and was used as a park for a herd of antelopes, while a limpid stream assured an abundant supply of water, even during the very hottest season.

There would thus be nothing to fear on the score of food for several months. Whether or not the two four-pounder carronades would be sufficient to repulse the flotilla if it made an attack in full force upon Shark's Island, nobody could say. The natives, of course, could have no knowledge of the power of these arms, whose reports would spread panic among them, not to mention the bullets and halls which the two guns and the carbines would rain upon them. But if even half of them succeeded in landing on the island there would be little hope.

There was not a moment to lose. Jack and Ernest brought round the boat to the mouth of Jackal River. Boxes of preserves, cassava, rice and flour, and also arms and ammunition were taken down to it. Then M. and Mme. Zermatt, Mr. and Mrs. Wolston, Ernest and Hannah got into it, while Jack took his seat in his canoe which would enable him, if need arose, to establish communication between the island and the shore. The animals, except the two dogs, had to be left at Rock Castle. The jackal, ostrich, and the onager were set at liberty. They would be able to find their own food.

The boat left the mouth of the river just as the pirogues came into sight off Whale Island. But it ran no risk of being seen in this portion of the sea lying between Rock Castle and Shark's Island.

Mr. Wolston and Ernest rowed, while M. Zermatt steered in such a way as to profit by certain backwaters which enabled them to make headway against the rising tide without excessive exertion. Nevertheless, for a mile they had to struggle hard not to be carried back towards Deliverance Bay, and it was three quarters of an hour before the boat slipped in among the rocks and anchored at the foot of the battery knoll.

They at once unloaded the chests, arms, and various articles brought from Rock Castle, which they deposited in the store-house. Mr. Wolston and Jack went to the battery, and took up their posts there to keep watch over the approaches to the island.

The flag flying from the signal mast was immediately pulled down. Nevertheless, it was to be feared that the savages had seen it, since their canoes were not more than a mile away. Thus they had to remain on the defensive in anticipation of an immediate attack.

The attack did not take place. When the pirogues were off the island, they turned southwards and the current took them in towards the mouth of Jackal River. After the savages had landed, the canoes were taken into shelter in the little creek where the pinnace lay at her moorings.

This was the position of affairs. For a fortnight the savages had been in possession of Rock Castle, and it did not appear that they had sacked the house. It was different at Falconhurst, and from the top of the knoll M. Zermatt had seen them chasing the animals, after they had wrought havoc in the rooms and store-houses.

But there was soon no doubt that the band had discovered that Shark's Island was serving as a refuge for the inhabitants of the island. On several occasions half-a-dozen of the canoes came across Deliverance Bay and made towards the island. Several shots sent among them by Ernest and Jack sank one or two and put the others to fight. But from that moment it was necessary to watch day and night. A night attack would be very difficult to repulse.

M. Zermatt hoisted the flag at the top of the hill again, for the improbable might happen, and a ship might come within sight of New Switzerland!

Chapter XV – Fighting For Life

The last hours of this night of the 24th of January '
conversation. The two families had so much to say, so many memories
to recall, so many fears for the future to discuss! No one thought of
going to sleep, except little Bob. But until daybreak M. Zermatt and his
companions did not relax their keen vigilance, relieving one another on
duty near the two cannonades, one loaded with ball, the other with
grape-shot.

Shark's Island was larger than Whale Island, which lay two and a half
miles away to the north, to the entrance to Flamingo Bay. It was an
oval, about half a mile long and a quarter of a mile across at its widest
part, thus having a circumference of something under two miles. By
day it had been comparatively easy to keep watch over it, and as it was
of the utmost importance that equally effective watch should be
maintained from sunset to sunrise, it was decided, on Captain Gould's
suggestion, that the whole of the shore should be patrolled.

Dawn came, and no alarm had been raised. Although the savages
knew that the island was held by a little garrison, they had no idea that
it had been reinforced and was in a position to offer them sterner
resistance. But it would not be long before they discovered that one of
their canoes had disappeared-that which bad taken Captain Gould and
his party from Falconhurst beach to Shark's Island.

"They may think," Fritz suggested, "that the canoe has been carried
away by the outgoing tide."

"Anyhow," M. Zermatt replied, "let us keep a careful lookout. As long
as the island is not invaded we have nothing to fear. Although there are
fifteen of us, we have plenty of food for a long time, with the reserves
in the storehouse, not to mention the herd of antelopes. The spring is
inexhaustible, and of ammunition we have enough, provided we are not
attacked very often."

"What the deuce!" John Block exclaimed.

"These tailless apes surely won't stay for ever on the island'

"Who can tell?" Mme. Zermatt answered.

ıf they have settled down in Rock Castle, they will never leave it. Oh! our poor dear house, prepared to receive all of you, my children, and now in their power!"

"Mother," said Jenny, "I do not think they have destroyed anything at Rock Castle, for they have no interest in doing so. We shall find our home in good condition, and we shall resume our life together there, and with the help of God-"

"Yes, of God," Frank added, "Who will not forsake us after having brought us all together again as by a miracle."

"Ah! If only I could work a miracle!" Jack exclaimed.

"What would you do, Mr. Jack?" the boatswain inquired.

"To begin with," the young man replied, "I would jolly well make these rascals decamp before they tried to land on this island, many of them as there are."

"And then?" Harry Gould asked.

"Then, captain, if they continued to infest our island with their presence, I would make either the *Unicorn* or another ship show its colors at the entrance to Deliverance Bay."

"But that would not be a miracle, Jack dear," Jenny said; "that is an event which will surely come to pass. One of these days we shall hear the guns saluting the new English colony."

"Why, it is surprising that no ship has come already!" Mr. Wolston agreed.

"Patience!" John Block replied. "Everything comes in its own good time."

"God grant it!" sighed Mme. Zermatt, whose confidence was shaken by her many trials.

And so, after having organized their life in New Switzerland, here were the two families brought down to making another start on a tiny islet, a mere annex to their island! How long would they be prisoners on it, and might they not fall into hostile hands if help did not reach them from outside?

The Castaways of the Flag

They proceeded to settle down for a stay perhaps of weeks, possibly even of months. As the store-house was large enough to accommodate fifteen people, Mme. Zermatt and Mrs. Wolston, Jenny, Susan, and her child, Hannah and Dolly were to sleep in the beds in the inner room while the men occupied the outer one.

Now, at the height of summer, the nights were warm, following the hot days. A few armfuls of grass dried in the sun were all that the men required, especially as they had to keep guard in turns, from evening until morning, upon the approaches to the island.

There was no occasion for anxiety with regard to the food supply. Of rice, tapioca, flour, smoked meat, and dried fish, such as salmon and herrings, the stores would suffice for the daily requirements of six months, without taking into account the fresh fish that could be caught at the foot of the rocks. The mangroves and palms on the island bore fruit in any quantity. There were two kegs of brandy to make an addition to the fresh and limpid water of the spring.

The only thing which might run short-and that possibility was serious-was ammunition, although they had brought some more over in the boat. If, as a consequence of repeated attacks, powder, bullets and cannon halls ran out, defense would cease to be possible.

While M. Zermatt and Ernest helped the women to make everything as comfortable as possible, Mr. Wolston and Captain Gould, the boatswain and Fritz and Jack and Frank surveyed Shark's Island on foot. Almost all round the coast it was easily accessible on little beaches lying between the projecting points of the coast-line. The best protected part was that commanded by the battery knoll, which rose at the south-west extremity, overlooking Deliverance Bay. At its foot there were enormous rocks, among which it would be very difficult to effect a landing. Everywhere else, light boats, such as these pirogues were, could find quite enough water to enable them to reach land. Consequently it was indispensable that they should keep all the approaches to the island under careful supervision.

In the course of their inspection Fritz and Frank had opportunity to observe the fine condition of the plantations. The mangroves, palms, and pines were in full fruit. Thick grass carpeted the pastures where the herd of antelopes capered and played. Many birds, flitting from tree to tree, filled the air with their myriad cries. The magnificent firmament poured light and warmth upon the surrounding sea.

The day after that on which the two families had taken refuge on the island, a bird arrived, to receive the warmest of welcomes. It was the albatross of Burning Rock, which Jenny had found again at Turtle Bay, and which had flown away from the top of Jean Zermatt peak in the direction of the Promised Land. When it arrived, the piece of thread that was still fastened round one of its legs attracted Jack's attention, and he caught the bird without any trouble. But, unfortunately, on this occasion, the albatross brought no tidings.

The men went up to the battery. From the top of the knoll an uninterrupted view could be obtained north as far as False Hope Point, east as far as Cape East, and south as far as the end of Deliverance Bay. To west, about two miles away, ran the long line of trees which bordered the shore between Jackal River and the Falconhurst woods. But they could not see whether the natives were roaming about

the Promised Land.

Just at this moment, at the mouth of Deliverance Bay, a few canoes came paddling out to sea, keeping well beyond range of the guns in the battery. By this time the savages had learned the danger of coming too near Shark's Island, and if they should attempt to land upon it they would most certainly wait for a very dark night.

Looking out to the open main in the northward, one saw nothing but deserted boundless space, and it was from that quarter that the *Unicorn,* or any other ship dispatched from England, must appear.

After having satisfied themselves that the battery was in order, the men were just preparing to come down, when Captain Gould asked:

"Is there not a powder magazine at Rock Castle?"

"Yes," Jack answered, "and I wish to goodness it were here instead of there! The three barrels that the *Unicorn* left us are in it."

"Where are they?"

"In a little cavity at the end of the orchard."

The boatswain guessed the captain's thought.

"Probably," he said, "those rascals may have discovered that magazine?"

"It is to be feared they may," Mr. Wolston answered.

"What is most to be feared," Captain Gould declared, "is that in their ignorance they may blow up the ho use."

"And themselves with it!" Jack exclaimed. "Well, if Rock Castle had to go to blazes in the explosion, it would be one solution, for I imagine that those left of the filthy creatures would decamp, without any heart to come back!"

Leaving the boatswain on sentry-go at the battery, the others went back to the storehouse. Breakfast was eaten together; how happy a meal it would have been if all the party had been gathered in the big hall at Rock Castle!

The next four days brought no change in the situation. Beyond keeping proper watch over the island, they did not know how to fill the long hours. How different everything would have been if the *Unicorn* had not been compelled to put in to Cape Town for repairs. They would all have been settled down at Rock Castle more than two months ago! And now that Fritz and Jenny were married, who could say that another wedding would not be celebrated soon, the union of Ernest and Hannah, which the corvette's chaplain might have blessed in the chapel of Rock Castle? There might have been whispers of a third union by and by-when Dolly should be eighteen.

Everyone fought bravely against despondency. As for John Block, he had lost none of his native good humor. They took long walks among the plantations. They watched Deliverance Bay, although no attack by the pirogues was to be apprehended while the sun was in the sky. Then, with night, all their anxiety returned, anticipating an attack in force.

So while the women retired within the second room of the store-house, the men made the rounds of the shore, ready to concentrate at the foot of the knoll if the enemy approached the island.

On the 29th of January, during the morning, there was still nothing unusual to be noted. The sun rose in a horizon undimmed by the faintest haze. The day would be very hot, and the light sea-breeze could hardly last until the evening.

Jules Verne

After the mid-day meal Captain Gould and Jack left the store and went to relieve Ernest and Mr. Wolston, who were on sentry-go at the battery.

Those two were just coming away when Captain Gould stopped them.

"There are several canoes at the mouth of Jackal River," he said.

"They are probably going fishing as usual," Jack replied. "They will take care to go by out of range of our guns."

Jack was scanning the place through the telescope.

"Ah!" he exclaimed." There are a lot of canoes this time. Wait: five, six, nine, and two more coming out of the creek; eleven, twelve! Can the whole fleet be going fishing?"

"Perhaps they are getting ready to attack us," Mr. Wolston said.

"We will be on our guard," said Captain Gould; "let us go and warn the others."

"Let us see first which way the canoes are going," Mr. Wolston replied.

"Anyhow, all our guns are ready," Jack added.

During the few hours that Jack had spent in the hands of the savages he had observed that their pirogues were in number fifteen, each able to carry seven or eight men. Twelve of these canoes could now be counted, rounding the point of the creek. With the help of the telescope they were able to calculate that the whole band of savages had gone aboard, and that there could not be a single aborigine remaining at Rock Castle.

"Can they be clearing out at last?" Jack exclaimed.

"It isn't very likely," Ernest answered. "More likely that they mean to pay a visit to Shark's Island."

"When does the ebb begin?" Captain Gould inquired.

"At half-past one," Mr. Wolston told him. "Then it will soon make itself felt, and as it will be in the favor of the canoes we shall then know what to expect."

The Castaways of the Flag

Ernest went to inform M. Zermatt, his brothers, and the boatswain, and all came and took up their posts under the hangar of the battery.

It was a little after one o'clock and, with the ebb only just beginning to run, the pirogues moved but slowly along the east coast. They kept as far away from the island as possible, in order to escape the projectiles whose range and power they now knew very well.

"Yet-suppose it were a final departure?' said Frank again.

"Then good luck to them and good-bye!" said Jack.

"And here's hoping we shall never see them back!" John Block added.

As yet no one would venture to prophesy such a happy contingency. Were not the canoes only waiting for the ebb to run strongly in order to make for the island?

Fritz and Jenny stood side by side, watching in silence, hardly daring to believe that the situation was drawing to so immediate an end.

It soon became apparent that the canoes were feeling the action of the out-going tide. Their speed increased, although they did not cease to hug the coast, as if it were the natives' intention to go round Cape East.

At half-past three the fleet was midway be-tween Deliverance Bay and Cape East. At six o'clock there could be no further doubt on the matter. The last boat rounded the cape and disappeared behind the point.

Neither M. Zermatt nor anyone else had left the knoll for a moment.

What relief was theirs when not a single pirogue remained in sight! At last the island was freed from the savages' presence! The whole party would be able to settle down in Rock Castle again. Perhaps there would be only trifling damage to make good. They would do nothing but watch for the arrival of the *Unicorn!* Their last fears were forgotten, and, after all, they were all together again after surviving so many dreadful trials!

"Shall we start for Rock Castle?" Jack exclaimed, eager to quit the island.

"Yes, yes!" said Dolly no less eagerly. Frank had just joined her.

"Would it not be better to wait until tomorrow?" Jenny suggested. "What do you think, Fritz dear?"

"What Mr. Wolston and Captain Gould and papa think," Fritz replied; "and that certainly is to spend this next night here."

"Yes," said M. Zermatt. "Before we return to Rock Castle we must be absolutely sure that the savages have no intention of going back there."

"They have gone to the devil already," Jack exclaimed, "and the devil never lets go of anything he has once got in his claws! Isn't that so, good old Block?"

"Yes-sometimes," the boatswain answered.

Despite Jack's protests and arguments, it was decided to postpone the start until the morrow, and all assembled at the last meal which they expected to take on Shark's Island.

It was a very merry one, and when the evening came to an end all were ready for bed.

Everything suggested that this night of the 29th of January would be as tranquil as the many others spent in the quietude of Rock Castle and Falconhurst.

Nevertheless, neither M. Zermatt nor his companions would depart from their customary caution, although all danger seemed to have gone with the last of the canoes. It was therefore arranged that some should make the usual nightly rounds while the others remained on guard at the battery.

As soon as the women and Bob had gone into the store, Jack, Ernest, Frank, and John Block, with their guns over their shoulders, set out to the north end of the island. Fritz and Captain Gould went up the knoll and took their place under the hangar, as it was their turn to go on guard until sunrise.

Mr. Wolston, M. Zermatt, and James stayed in the store, where they were free to sleep until dawn.

The night was a dark one, with no moon. The atmosphere was thick with the evaporations from the heated earth. The breeze had fallen at evening. Profound silence reigned. Nothing was audible save the surf of the incoming tide, which began to flow about eight o'clock.

Harry Gould and Fritz sat side by side, recalling memories of all the events, good and ill, that had followed each other after the *Flag* had cast them adrift. From time to time one or other of them went out and looked carefully about, more especially in the direction of the dark arm of the sea lying between the two capes.

Nothing disturbed their utter solitude until, at two o'clock in the morning, the captain and Fritz were startled out of their conversation by a report.

"A gun!" said Harry Gould.

"Yes, fired over there," Fritz answered, pointing to the north-west of the island.

"What's up, then?"

Captain Gould exclaimed. Both rushed out of the hangar and peered for any light in the midst of the profound darkness.

Two other reports rang out, nearer this time than the first one.

"The canoes have come back," said Fritz.

And leaving Harry Gould at the battery he ran to the store at top speed.

M. Zermatt and Mr. Wolston had heard the reports, and were already on the threshold.

"What is the matter?" M. Zermatt asked sharply.

"I am afraid, papa, that the savages have tried to effect a landing," Fritz answered.

"And the rascals have succeeded!" exclaimed Jack, who now approached with Ernest and the boatswain.

"They are on the island!" said Mr. Wolston. "Their canoes touched the north-east point just at the very moment we got there," said Ernest, "and our shots were not enough to frighten them off. And now nothing remains but-"

"To defend ourselves!" Captain Gould finished for him.

The ladies had just left their room. In anticipation of an immediate attack they had to carry all the arms, ammunition and stores they could, and get to the battery as quickly as possible.

The departure of the pirogues had been merely a ruse. Taking advantage of the incoming tide, the savages had returned towards Shark's Island, which they hoped to take by surprise. The manoeuvre had been highly successful. Although their presence was known and they had been welcomed with guns, they were in occupation of the point, whence it would be easy for them to get to the central store.

The situation was thus desperate, for the pirogues had succeeded in landing the entire band. M. Zermatt and his companions could not offer a serious resistance to so large a number of assailants. That they must succumb when their ammunition and supplies ran out was only too certain.

They could do nothing but take refuge on the knoll, within the battery. That was the only place where there was any possibility of putting up a defense.

The women and Bob crept under cover in the hangar which sheltered the two guns. They did not let a murmur escape them.

For one moment M. Zermatt thought of carrying them over to the Falconhurst shore in the boat. But what would become of the unfortunate women if, after the islet had been invaded, their companions were unable to join them? Besides, they would never have consented to go.

It was a little after four o 'clock when a confused noise announced the presence of the savages, a couple of hundred yards away. Captain Gould, M. Zermatt, Mr. Wolston, Ernest, Frank, James, and the boatswain, armed with carbines, were ready to fire, while Fritz and Jack stood with matches lighted near the two little cannon, only waiting for the moment to rake the slopes of the knoll with grape-shot.

When the black shadows showed against the early light of dawn, Captain Gould gave the order in a low tone to fire in that direction. Seven or eight reports rang out, followed by horrible cries which proved that more than one bullet had found its billet in the crowd.

The Castaways of the Flag

Three attacks had to be repelled before sunrise. In the last a score or so of natives succeeded in reaching the crest of the knoll. Although some of them had been mortally hit, the carbines could no longer keep them in check, and but for a double discharge of the ordnance the battery would probably have been carried in this assault.

At daylight the band withdrew among the trees, near the store, as if they meant to wait until the next night to renew the attack.

Unfortunately the defenders had almost exhausted their cartridges. When they were reduced to the two guns, which could only be directed towards the base of the knoll, how could they cover the summit?

A council was held to consider the situation. If they could not carry on the resistance under these conditions, would it not be possible to leave Shark's Island, land on Falconhurst beach, and seek refuge within the Promised Land or in some other part of the island all of them together, this time? Or would it be better to make a rush on the savages and, with the advantage of carbines over bows and arrows, compel them to take to the sea again? But M. Zermatt and his party were only nine against the scores who surrounded the knoll.

Just at this moment, as if in answer to this last suggestion, the air was filled with the whistling of arrows, some of which stuck in the roof of the hangar, fortunately without wounding anyone.

"The attack is beginning again!" said John Block.

"Let's get ready for them!" Fritz replied.

This assault was the fiercest of all, for the natives were furious, and seemed no longer afraid to face the bullets and grape-shot. Moreover, the ammunition was almost exhausted, and the fire slackened. Several of the savages crawled up the knoll and got to the hangar. The two carronades fired point blank at them, cleared the ground of a few, and Fritz, Jack, Frank, James, and John Block fought hand to hand with the others. Then they retired over the corpses which strewed the foot of the hill. They had used a weapon between axe and club, which, in their hands, was a formidable thing.

Plainly the struggle approached its end. The last cartridges were spent. Numbers must tell. M. Zermatt and his party were trying to make a stand around the hangar, which must soon be entered. At grips with

Jules Verne

several natives, Fritz and Frank and Jack and Harry Gould were in imminent peril of being borne down to the foot of the hill. The fight would be over in a few minutes now, and defeat meant massacre, for they could expect no mercy from these savage foes.

Just at this moment a report rang out off the island, borne by the wind from the north.

The assailants heard it, for those in advance stopped.

Fritz and Jack and the others at once ran back towards the hangar, one or two of them slightly wounded.

"A gun!" Frank exclaimed.

"And a gun from a ship-or I'm a Dutchman!" the boatswain declared.

"There is a ship in sight," said M. Zermatt.

"It is the *Unicorn,*" Jenny replied.

"And it's God who has sent her now!" Frank murmured.

The echoes of Falconhurst rang with a second detonation, much closer, and the savages recoiled into cover under the trees.

Jack sprang to the flag-staff, and, nimble as any top-man, scrambled to the top of it.

"Ship! Ship ahoy!" he yelled.

All eyes were turned towards the north.

Above False Hope Point the top-sails of a ship appeared, swelling in the morning breeze.

A three-master, on the port tack, was manoeuvring to get round the point, which thereafter was known as Cape Deliverance.

From her mizzen-mast flew the flag of Great Britain!

The women appeared stretching their hands to heaven in ardent gratitude.

"What about those ruffians?" Fritz inquired.

"They're running!" replied Jack, who had just slid down the flag-staff.

The Castaways of the Flag

"Yes, they're running!" John Block added.

"And if they don't clear jolly quick, we'll help them along with our last four-pounders."

And indeed, surprised by the detonations ringing from the north, scared by the sight of the ship coming round the point, the savages had fled to the point where their canoes were lying. They clambered into them, shoved off hard and paddled vigorously in the direction of Cape East.

The boatswain and Jack went back into the hangar and trained the two guns upon them; and three canoes, cut in half, went to the bottom.

Just as the ship, coming under full sail into the arm of the sea, was off Shark's Island, she joined her heavy guns to those of the battery. Most of the pirogues failed to escape the rain of shot and shell, and only two succeeded in vanishing behind the cape, never to return.

Jules Verne

Chapter XVI – Conclusion

It actually was the *Unicorn* which had just dropped anchor at the mouth of Deliverance Bay. All the repairs effected, Captain Littlestone had left Cape Town after a stay of several months, and at last had reached New Switzerland, of which he was to take official possession in the name of England.

Captain Littlestone now learned from Captain Gould's lips the events of which the *Flag* had been the stage.

As for what had become of that vessel, whether Robert Borupt was playing pirate in the ill-famed waters of the Pacific, or whether he and his accomplices had perished in some furious tornado was destined never to be known, and was of little consequence to the islanders.

It was an immense satisfaction to the two families when they found that the dwelling at Rock Castle had not been sacked. The natives had probably contemplated taking up their quarters there, intending to settle on the island. There was no damage done to the bed-rooms or halls, no sign of pillage in the outhouses or stores, no havoc in the orchard or adjoining fields.

They recovered all the domestic animals which had scattered in the neighborhood, the buffaloes Storm and Grumbler, the ostrich Whirlwind, the monkey Nip, the onager Lightfoot, the cow Paleface and her meadow companions, the bull Roarer and his stable companions, the asses Swift, Arrow, and Dart, the jackal, and Jenny's albatross, which had flown across the arm of the sea between Shark's Island and Rock Castle.

As it could not be very long before several ships dispatched from England would arrive with colonists and their stores, it became necessary to choose the site for new buildings.

It was decided that these should be erected along the banks of Jackal River, up towards the fall. Rock Castle would thus be the first village of the colony, pending the time when it should have grown into a town. No doubt in the future it would rank as the capital of New Switzerland, for it would be the most important of the little towns which would grow up in the heart of the Promised Land, and beyond.

The Castaways of the Flag

The *Unicorn* was under orders to remain in Deliverance Bay until the emigrants arrived. So animation reigned along the coast from

Three weeks had not elapsed before a ceremony, which it was agreed to make as brilliant as possible, brought together Commander Littlestone and the officers and crew of his ship, Captain Harry Gould and the boatswain, and all the members of the Zermatt and Wolston families, now to be united to one another in still closer bonds.

On that day the chaplain of the *Unicorn* celebrated in the chapel of Rock Castle the marriage of Ernest Zermatt and Hannah Wolston. It was the first wedding on the island of New Switzerland, but the future would no doubt see it followed by many others.

And, in point of fact, two years later, Frank became the husband of Dolly Wolston. On this occasion it was not in the humble chapel that the pastor of the colony gave his blessing to the happy pair. The ceremony was held in a church erected midway between Rock Castle and Falconhurst, in the avenue. The steeple, rising above the trees, was visible three miles out to sea.

No need to dilate further upon the progress of New Switzerland! The fortunate isle saw the number of its inhabitants increasing every year. Deliverance Bay, well protected from the winds and waves, offered excellent anchorage for ships, and among these the pinnace *Elizabeth* cut no bad figure.

Regular communication with England was established. This inaugurated a most profitable export trade. By that time there were four more villages, Wood Grange, Sugar-cane Grove, Eberfurt, and Prospect Hill. A harbor was made at the mouth of the Montrose River, and another at Unicorn Bay, the latter connected with Deliverance Bay by a good carriage road.

Three years after New Switzerland had been taken possession of by England her population exceeded two thousand. The British government had left the colony her autonomy, and M. Zermatt was elected to the position of Governor of New Switzerland. Heaven grant that his successors may be as good as that excellent and worthy man!

A detachment of troops from India garrisoned the island after fortifications had been constructed at Cape East and Cape Deliverance (formerly known as False Hope Point), so as to command the arm of the sea which gave access to Deliverance Bay.

Of course, this had nothing to do with any fear of savages, neither those of the Andamans and Nicobars, nor those of the Australian coast. But New Switzerland's position in these waters, besides offering excellent anchorage for ships, was of real importance from a strategic point of view at the entrance to the Sunda Seas and the Indian Ocean. It was only proper, therefore, that it should be provided with means of defense.

Such is the complete history of this island from the day when a storm cast a father, mother and four children upon it. For twelve years that brave and intelligent family worked without ceasing, and set in operation all the energy of a virgin soil, which was rendered fruitful by the magic climate of the tropic regions. And so their prosperity had never ceased to grow nor their welfare to be increased, until the day when the arrival of the *Unicorn* enabled them to establish relations with the rest of the world.

As has been related, a second family voluntarily threw in its fortune with theirs, and materially and morally existence was never happier than in the fertile domain of the Promised Land.

Then began a period of severe trial. Ill fortune fell upon these good people. They knew the fear of never seeing again those for whom they were waiting, and the peril of being attacked by a horde of savages!

But even in the darkest hours of that unhappy time they never lost faith in Providence. Then at last bright days returned, and never again are dark ones to be feared for the second fatherland of the two families.

And now New Switzerland is flourishing and will soon be too small to receive all those who are attracted to her. Her commerce is finding outlets in Europe as well as in Asia, thanks to the proximity of Australia, India, and the Netherlands possessions. Most fortunately the nuggets found in the gorge by the Montrose River proved to be very rare, and the colony was not invaded by gold-seekers, who usually leave nothing but disorder and misery in their train!

The marriages which united the Zermatt and Wolston families have been blessed by Heaven. The grandparents will soon feel that they live again in their grandchildren. Only Jack is content with the nephews and

162

nieces who clamber on his knees. He said he was a born uncle, and in that relation was certainly a great success.

Though the island now forms part of the colonial dominions of Great Britain, it has been allowed to retain its name of New Switzerland in honor of the Zermatt family.

The End